FERGUSON'S FERRY

Also by Noel Loomis
in Large Print:

Above the Palo Duro
Heading West

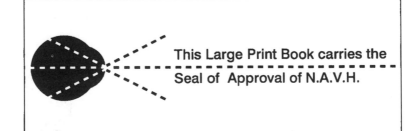

This Large Print Book carries the
Seal of Approval of N.A.V.H.

Ferguson's Ferry

Noel Loomis

G.K. Hall & Co. • Thorndike, Maine

Copyright, ©, 1962, by Noel Loomis.

All rights reserved.

Published in 2001 by arrangement with Golden West
Literary Agency

G.K. Hall Large Print Western Series.

The text of this Large Print edition is unabridged.
Other aspects of the book may vary from the original edition.

Set in 16 pt. Plantin by Myrna S. Raven.

Printed in the United States on permanent paper.

Library of Congress Cataloging-in-Publication Data

Loomis, Noel M., 1905–
    Ferguson's ferry / by Noel Loomis.
      p.   cm.
     ISBN 0-7838-9410-4 (lg. print : hc : alk. paper)
     1. Ferryboat captains — Fiction   2. Missouri River —
Fiction.   3. Ferries — Fiction.   4. Large type books.
I. Title.
PS3523.O554 F47 2001
  813'.54—dc21   00-143881

FERGUSON'S FERRY

CHAPTER I

THE LATE JUNE sun was blazing in Nebraska. The wind that rolled across the interminable leagues of tightly-curled buffalo grass drove before it a smothering heat that made the horned toads rest in the scant shade of dust-laden sagebrush or sun-shriveled prickly pear. But the white-topped wagons kept lumbering from the East. They came from Illinois, Indiana, Ohio, Pennsylvania. The long lines converged at Omaha City, at the eastern edge of Nebraska, to cross the Missouri River. A few of the bearded, booted emigrants took a second look at the black soil of Iowa and decided they had come far enough, but more of them had that absent look of the far distance in their eyes, and were not deterred by the long, long miles that lay ahead, by the prospect of bone-dry prairie and burned-out grass, of buffalo chips for fuel and rattlesnakes for food, of Indians grimly determined to take scalps, of babies conceived and babies delivered in the jolting wagons, of brutal fights, of tragic deaths, of graves marked only by the tears of those who could not stay to mourn — graves obliterated by the rolling wheels of heavy wagons to hide the bodies from the Indians.

In the year of 1857, thousands upon endless thousands of the gray-canvassed vehicles pulled

7

up at the mighty river, and sometimes the trampled grass was covered with oxen for miles back as the booted emigrants awaited their turn at the overloaded ferries. But some families, already worn by the long, hard trip, impatiently spread down the river from Omaha City to look for other rumored ferries, and some followed the stream up-river, coming at last to the busy ferry of Sandy John Ferguson. Some, passing up the green hills of Iowa for the fabled rich soil of Oregon, paid for their passage in gold, and went on west over the rolling hills. Others, more intent on extracting money wherever they might and by whatever means they could devise, saw opportunities closer at hand. And not infrequently a sharp-eyed man, recognizing the value of the ferry itself, began to test his power against Ferguson as soon as he could. . . .

Ferguson was Irish, with a slight but pleasant brogue. He was tall and lanky, white-skinned and red-haired, and likely to be taken for a highland Scot rather than a Dubliner. He took a turn around a fence-post, up on the bank, with the rope that held the ferry steady in its mooring-place on the Nebraska side of the river, and waited for a heavy-set man in knee-high boots to stride from the ferry onto the small floating pier.

The heavy-set man stomped on the thick boards and glared at a group of men on the bank. "Where's Ferguson?" he demanded.

Sandy John straightened up. "I'm Ferguson," he said.

The stranger looked at him importantly. "I am Henry Wiggins."

Ferguson nodded slightly, his eyes on the man, but said nothing.

Wiggins waved his arms as if his patience was about at an end. "I have waited on the other side since yesterday morning to ride this flimsy pile of logs."

Bill Benson came down the river bank where he had tied the span of mules that had pulled the ferry to the Nebraska side. He stopped a little above Wiggins, looked at Ferguson, and waited.

Ferguson sighed. He had operated the ferry until two o'clock that morning before he had closed down for a wink of sleep — and still the sun would not be up for another half hour. But he looked at Wiggins from the snubbing-post and said quietly, "This is the west side, Mr. Wiggins."

Wiggins snorted. "What's the price?"

"The fare is two dollars, gold or silver," said Ferguson, walking down a short, muddy incline.

Wiggins held out a piece of green paper. "Here's five on the Bank of Nemaha."

Ferguson regarded him steadily. "I said gold or silver, Mr. Wiggins."

The heavier man looked at him with his shoe-button eyes and said challengingly, "I am

9

told the Bank of Nemaha is good."

Bill Benson moved a little closer. The men above spread out, and beyond them a big plowhorse thundered up at a clumsy trot and came to a stop, tossing his head while a woman slid down from a sidesaddle.

"The Bank of Nemaha," Ferguson said, "never was a bank. Its only function was to act as a name for the issuance of money."

The woman started down the sloping bank, raising her skirts a little to avoid tripping.

Wiggins began to swell up. "You're telling me this money is no good?" he demanded.

"I am telling you nothing," said Ferguson, "except that the ferry price is in gold or silver."

The woman came to a stop ten feet above them, watching. Major Yeakel, the mortgage agent, left a big walnut tree where he had been talking with the people from the first three wagons that morning, and came toward Ferguson and Wiggins, followed by the men from the wagons, one of whom looked back and said, "Now, Mrs. Talbot, this here is man trouble. You stay back and keep your ears covered."

Wiggins looked up and seemed to take assurance from the gathering audience. "You're takin' it on yourself to pass judgment on the banks of Nebraska, Mr. Ferguson?"

Ferguson would not be diverted. "You do not like this ferry, Mr. Wiggins?"

Wiggins glared at him. "You're a highway robber," he said.

10

"At Omaha City the fare is four dollars," said Ferguson.

A black-haired man named Jones, who had ferried over a wagon the night before, and who had been talking to the newspaper editor as to whether he should go farther west or take up a claim right there, came slowly down the bank followed by half a dozen others, and now the river bank bore a scattered semi-circle of men, with the woman a little in front of them.

Ferguson looked at the woman on the bank, then at another woman still sitting on the seat of the wagon on the ferry; so far, the second woman had not made a move or a sound. He looked back at the older man. "You are a hard man to get an answer from, Mr. Wiggins."

Wiggins took in the audience with his quick eyes, and made a grandstand play. "I don't like your ferry and I don't like you," he said at last.

Ferguson appeared unmoved. "Your feeling for me, Mr. Wiggins, can be overlooked, but your dislike of my ferry is a personal matter that I cannot accept lightly."

"What the hell are you drivin' at?" Wiggins asked, suddenly suspicious.

Ferguson explained. "I am licensed by the territory of Nebraska to operate a ferry at this point, and I —"

"I heard. I also heard that the first men into the territory made a run for the ferries — like bankers — and grabbed everything in sight,

11

and now they squeeze the last drop of blood out of everybody who comes along."

Ferguson's blue eyes were bleak. "The fare, Mr. Wiggins, is two dollars, gold or silver."

"I won't pay it."

The woman came another step down the bank, and stopped. Ferguson glanced at her. In the early dawn, she was young and pretty; under the sunbonnet her white face was framed by black hair, and set off by dark eyes that seemed unaccountably concerned. Ferguson said, "You'd best stay back, Mrs. Talbot. There may be trouble."

She stopped. "Mr. Ferguson, I am no stranger to trouble — as you should know since you killed my husband."

Wiggins took one step toward him, holding out the Bank of Nemaha currency. "Are you accepting this, Mr. Ferguson?"

Ferguson did not look away from Wiggins and he did not raise his voice. "Cast off the rope, Mr. Benson."

Bill Benson loosened the double half-hitch, lifted off the rope, coiled it in a swift motion and tossed it onto the deck of the ferry. Up on the bank beyond the men, the span of mules, their chain unsnapped from the towing rope, were snipping up a few blades of coarse grass. From the opposite shore (the Iowa side), through the swirls of mist that still moved ghostlike over the water, came the sound of reins slapping on animals' hips. A chain

12

snapped across the river, the rope creaked, and the log ferry began to move back toward the east.

The woman sitting in the wagon on the ferry showed the first sign of life, and began to clamber down over the wheel. The two pairs of oxen stayed where they were, one ox standing, three lying, all placidly chewing their cuds. The woman stepped on the axle, then, looking behind, she saw the water going by for the first time and clambered hurriedly back to the seat. "Henry!" she screamed, "Henry! Help!"

The ferry moved steadily toward the east side through the swirls of mist. Wiggins stared for a moment, then charged Ferguson, who moved only a little — but enough. Wiggins, the heavier of the two, went on by, floundered for an instant and then straightened up as Ferguson's fist caught him at the corner of his chin. He aimed a roundhouse blow at Ferguson, who evaded it. He aimed another, this one catching Ferguson on the side of the head. Ferguson weaved for a moment, but managed to hammer his bony fists into Wiggins' face.

Wiggins began to puff. He stood slightly above Ferguson, and stopped for a moment to appeal to the sympathy of the crowd, which, by that time, had grown to thirty or forty — all men but Mrs. Talbot. "I heard about him all the way across Ioway," Wiggins said, and turned. "You been collecting your pound of flesh from everybody who comes this way."

"I collect nothing unless they wish to use my ferry," said Ferguson.

"But if they have no money —"

"You have money," said Ferguson. "You also have friends, for you have been across the river for two days, trying to work up feeling against me." He glanced at the men beyond Wiggins. "Are any of your friends in that bunch?"

Nobody answered and Ferguson said sharply, "Mr. Simmons?"

Simmons was a short man, heavy-set. His eyes smouldered, and he said harshly, "We'll all fry our own fish, John Ferguson, in our own good time — and we'll have some to fry," he added.

Ferguson's eyes lingered on the man for a second. Simmons had tried to buy a half-interest in the ferry, but Ferguson had refused, and now he had no doubt that Simmons would try to get it some other way. Ferguson glanced then at Major Scott, and saw his apparent neutrality. He looked beyond Scott, and said: "Mr. Logan, are you here in the interest of news, or are you prepared to take sides?"

Charlie Logan said, "I come to see what was about to happen."

"I have never seen you out so early," Ferguson observed.

Charlie Logan, a spare man with a black beard went on. "I did have news there was gonna be a showdown."

"I have some things to talk to you about,"

14

said Ferguson, "as soon as I get the ferry going."

"I'll be in my office all day soon as I get back."

"A showdown," Ferguson said softly, and looked at Wiggins. "It is to be a showdown, Mr. Wiggins — with the editor of the *Chronicle* in full attendance, having come eleven miles on horseback from Chippewa City. You must have felt sure of yourself, Mr. Wiggins."

Wiggins leaped suddenly downhill. Ferguson jumped out of the way, and Wiggins' momentum made it hard for him to turn. He tried to stop, but slipped in the mud and went down on his coattails, sliding. He clutched at the floating pier, but his fingers failed to get a hold on the wet wood, and he went into brown water with a great splash. Mrs. Wiggins screamed. "Help! He can't swim!"

Ferguson watched Wiggins flounder ashore in three feet of water.

"You tried to kill him!" The ferry was steadily drawing away, and her last words sounded reedy as she tried to raise her voice.

The tall Irishman looked up and smiled gently in the dawn. "Madam," he said in that carrying voice. "I am sorry only that such a beautiful lady as yourself is married to such a man as this." He looked down to where Wiggins was climbing up the muddy incline on hands and knees. "If you do not want to swim back," he said coldly to Wiggins, "you'd best catch the ferry before it gets into deep water."

Wiggins looked up, his face red. "You rawhided the wrong man," he said harshly.

Ferguson said without rancor but without bending: "I have encountered the right man, Mr. Wiggins. I have heard much about you. You are a professional squatter and a land speculator, and you have been camped on yon side of the river for some days, making your plans."

Wiggins was on the floating pier, and now he stood up, muddy and dripping, and his anger was not pleasant to behold.

"I paid you —" he began.

"You have paid me nothing," said Ferguson.

"I call on all these men to witness that I tendered you payment at the legal rate."

The pulley that ran along the rope to keep the ferry from drifting downstream, began to screech.

"Not in the legal tender," said Ferguson, and his eyes suddenly narrowed. "I have been running this ferry for a long time and I have seen some unpleasant men cross this river — but all have paid."

Wiggins stared at him. "All right, you win," he said suddenly. "Bring the wagon back, and I'll give you the money in gold."

But Ferguson said coldly, "The ferry is halfway across the river. It will cost you three dollars now, Mr. Wiggins."

Wiggins said with a growl in his voice, "You'll push me too far."

Ferguson said, "I know how far I can push you, Mr. Wiggins. I have had an opportunity to judge many men since I have been here."

Wiggins' eyes narrowed. "Where do you place me?"

Ferguson said calmly: "You are the kind who tries in many ways to be a big man but who always seems to fall short."

He must have hit Wiggins in a tender spot, for the man stood for a moment without change of expression. Then his eyes hardened, and once again he made the decision that he must have made many times: to be bold and aggressive. He pulled a butcher knife from inside his shirt and, with blade glistening, rushed at Ferguson.

Ferguson went in under the raised knife-arm, his left hand seeking the man's wrist. He tried to throw him over backward, but Wiggins hunched himself close to the ground and pushed up with all his strength.

Somehow, Ferguson succeeded in wrenching the knife from Wiggins, only to have it knocked suddenly from his grasp. Wiggins went to his knees, took hold of Ferguson's ankles with his hands, and arose fast with his head in Ferguson's belly. When he reached his full height, with powerful arms and shoulders he lifted Ferguson's legs straight up, and Ferguson, already off balance, went face forward over Wiggins' back toward the ground.

Wiggins gave him a last mighty shove, and

Ferguson fell, spread-eagled, and crashed against the edge of the floating pier. It caved in his ribs and knocked the wind out of his lungs, and he felt his consciousness go for a moment. Then he reacted to the chill of the water as he fell in headfirst.

He sprawled out flat, but got his feet on the mud bottom, and stood up to gasp for air. He turned to grasp the pier and start up, but Wiggins stomped on one hand with his heel. Ferguson felt the pain like a hammer-blow, and heard the boot-nails grind against his fingers, then jerked away his hand, staring at the bloody fingers stiff and straight before him. Then the same crashing pain came in his left hand, and he knew it also had been stomped.

He jerked it away, again seeing the fingers straight and bleeding before him.

Wiggins, having retrieved his butcher knife, waited at the edge of the pier. Ferguson was waist-deep in the muddy water. He had a hunting knife inside his shirt, but he did not know whether he could hold it, for his fingers were numb. He waited a moment, wondering if perhaps Wiggins would come after him — but Wiggins waited too.

Ferguson went slowly to one side of the pier. As he rounded the corner, for an instant out of Wiggins' sight, he reached down into the water and got both hands full of mud. Then he straightened and went toward shore at a wide angle from the pier.

Wiggins moved to meet him, and Ferguson would have to climb a two-foot mud bank to get on solid footing. He stopped at a distance from the water line.

Wiggins looked triumphant as he got set above him.

Ferguson started forward, but saw the butcher knife swinging in an arc for his throat. He ducked and backed away, trying to tempt Wiggins to fall into the water with him.

But Wiggins had an advantage and knew it. He waited for Ferguson to come within his reach.

Ferguson took a step toward the shore. Wiggins balanced on the balls of his feet. Ferguson leaned in, and Wiggins swung the knife. Ferguson swept his right arm around, and the handful of mud landed squarely in Wiggins' face. Ferguson leaped out of the water, found footing, and turned to grapple.

Wiggins scraped the mud away so he could see. The knife came at Ferguson, and went through shirt and skin and slid along his ribs before it found an open space and went through. But the force of the blow was fairly well spent, and it did not go deep. Ferguson jerked away, snatched the man's arm with both hands, and broke the forearm over his knee with a savage crack of splintered bones.

The knife dropped into the mud, but Wiggins uttered a strangled cry and rushed at him, his right arm hanging useless.

19

Ferguson saw the madness in his face. He stepped aside, and hit the man with his shoulder as Wiggins went by, trying to turn. Wiggins caromed off like a billiard ball, and fell on his face at the edge of the water. He rolled over and bounded up, and came back, insane with rage. Ferguson stepped in and hit him in the face, again and again, with all the power of his long muscles. The bones cracked in his hands, but he kept swinging until Wiggins went down and sprawled out, limp.

Ferguson turned to the men around him in a semi-circle, rubbing mud from between his fingers. "Mr. Simmons," he said, "do you want to claim him?"

Simmons glowered, and Ferguson knew that some day Simmons too would have to be whipped. Simmons said slowly, "I will see that he gets back across the river."

Charlie Logan, the editor, came up. "John Ferguson, what do you aim to do now?"

Ferguson looked at him. "Is there any call for me to do anything but wait for the next ruffian?"

Logan eyed him. "You know what they will say, don't you?"

Bill Benson brought the mules back and snapped the chain into a ring at the end of the rope, which was no longer moving.

Ferguson took a full breath. "What will they say?"

"They will say that you grabbed this ferry license when you first came to Nebraska, that you have made a fortune from it, that you have killed three men and beaten a dozen others to keep anybody else from interferin'."

Ferguson straightened to his full height. "What is wrong with that — I mean having a license and making money?" he asked.

Charlie Logan backed away a step. "They might say that you think you're God, decidin' who can come acrost and who can't."

Ferguson looked at him. "Would *you* say that, Mr. Logan?"

"Well, I — Lookie here, John Ferguson. You're a fine scrapper and otherwise you mind your own business — but this kind of thing has happened too often."

Ferguson turned on them all. "And it has happened," he said, "because the crooked land-grabbers and professional squatters and fake townsite promoters have heard that Ferguson's Ferry is the place to come to steal land from the government, and you, Mr. Logan, have done nothing to discourage that report with your wild-eyed editorials in the *Chronicle*, and they try to pass off worthless paper instead of paying in gold or silver." He swung on the mortgage agent, "And you, Major Yeakel, have done nothing to discourage it, for you make a commission on every loan, good or bad. And you, Mr. Logan, print four thousand papers every week and send them back East, and they are paid for by the Western Massachusetts Emigrant Aid Society, and you have not the moral courage to oppose these goings-on because it might stop people from coming out here. And you, Mr. Simmons, with your talk of getting a townsite charter from the territorial legislature. Every one of you would like to see me disposed of because I am the only one this side of Omaha will tell emigrants the truth." He looked back at the newspaperman. "So let them talk, Mr. Logan. Let them say what they will. As long as I own this ferry, I will continue to operate it as honestly as I know how, and also continue to give the straight facts to the emigrants." He raked them all with his blue eyes. "I am coming to see you this afternoon, gentlemen. You especially, Mr. Logan."

The newspaperman backed away a step. "What do you want to see me for?"

"At the rate rowdies and thieves are coming in, they will soon overrun us, and I am going to organize a Ferguson's Ferry Protective Claim Association, Mr. Logan, and I want you to announce it in your paper. If there is no law in this part of the territory, we will make some law. If men like Wiggins are allowed to come in and are welcomed with open arms, with none to oppose them, an honest man will not be able to live here for thirty days."

Simmons, tying up Wiggins' forearm, looked at Ferguson. "That claim association is illegal," he said. "It's just a way to get around the law. We'll fight it."

"Of course you will," said Ferguson, "and it will be a fight to see if honest people can keep men like you from sticking their noses in the public feed-trough at everybody else's expense."

Simmons exploded and came at him. Ferguson was weary by that time and beginning to weaken, but he stepped aside from Simmons' floundering rush, went after him, seized his left arm as Simmons was turning, and pivoted to his own left, bringing Simmons' arm across his back until he heard it crack. Simmons roared, and the men closed in silently.

Simmons' face was white, and the men muttered as they helped him away.

Major Yeakel looked at Ferguson curiously. "A bone-breaker," he said. "That's mayhem, Ferguson — mayhem."

Ferguson held his left arm close against his side. "I don't seem to have any friends at Ferguson's Ferry," he said, "and I don't suppose I shall — until we get a few honest men in the neighborhood."

CHAPTER II

FERGUSON WALKED UPSTREAM to a clump of willows, went behind it, and took off his shirt. It was a fairly deep wound, but he did not think it had hit his lung. He got down on his knees to wash it. He heard steps, and Mr. Benson appeared. "Need any help?" he asked.

"Guess not," said Ferguson. The wound was already turning blue around the edges of the cut. "He had a dull knife," Ferguson noted. "He is the kind who *would* have."

"He would have had a broken back," Benson said, "if you had not taken pity on him."

Ferguson grunted as he got the wound thoroughly clean.

"I brung the axle grease," said Benson, pulling up the lid of the can with his nails.

Ferguson smeared it on liberally, while Benson tore a strip from an old red shirt that had been rolled up under his arm. They tied it around Ferguson's chest.

No Horse, the Oto Indian who helped Benson, came down with the span of mules and expertly tied the end of the towrope to the rung on the doubletrees.

Ferguson looked at Benson. He was a mild little fellow, older than the usual emigrant — getting close to sixty, Ferguson thought — and he was the kind they always picked on.

"I lost my farm in Missouri to the tax collector," Benson said, rolling up the rest of the red shirt, "and I figured to come out here where land was free, and start all over." He drew a deep breath. "But a feller like Simmons don't care who gets there first. He got my hundred and sixty."

He followed Ferguson's eyes. "It looks like we got a covered wagon with a whole passel of young'uns, this time."

"And an extra man with a black horse," Ferguson noted. "Dressed in deerskin and moccasins. Long black hair. A mountain man, maybe?"

Benson shook his head. "I was with Ashley when he fought the 'Rees, and I knowed Smith and Bridger and Leroux and the lot, and I never seen a mountain man walk like that."

"Like what?"

"So all-fired open and biggety — like he was expectin' the wimmen to come flockin' around him."

Ferguson's eyes narrowed slightly. "Lots of different kinds come across on the ferry."

Benson nodded vigorously. "That there ferry is the key to the whole thing, Johnny. You can keep tabs on who comes into the country — and it's the only thing around here that's good for reg'lar cash money."

"I was lucky to get here first," Ferguson admitted.

Benson stared at him. "You'll be lucky to

keep it," he said. "Them fellers are full of schemes, and they won't rest until they git control of the crossin'."

Ferguson hitched up his trousers as he started back. "That may be a while," he said.

Ferguson walked out on the dock and called across the water to the figure in deerskins, who now stood with his feet apart, a long-barreled Kentucky rifle held upright in his left hand.

"Throw the snubbing-rope," said Ferguson.

The man did not move. "I paid six bits for passage on this boat," said the man. "I didn't hire on as a deck hand."

Ferguson ran out to the end of the dock and jumped the gap without trouble. Mr. Benson could almost bring her in with his mules. Ferguson sprang to the stern, cast the coil of rope to the dock, and leaped off again. He caught up the end of the rope, passed it around the snubbing-post, and brought a little pressure against it as the stern passed him. The rope creaked and the ferry slowed.

"All right, Mr. Benson," Ferguson called in that voice that did not have to be raised.

The towrope went slack. Ferguson put on more pressure and brought the ferry to a dead stop. The front end swung in slowly against the dock. He took a double half-hitch on the post, and then stepped across onto the ferry and ran up to the bow to get the forward rope. He secured it on the forward snubbing-post, and finally straightened up and looked at the man in deerskin clothing. He wore a very broad black hat with no sag in the brim — which marked him as a newcomer immediately. Ferguson said, "You can pay me the six bits."

"Your price is high," said the man, who was not over thirty.

"You agreed to it," said Ferguson, wary.

The man gave him a silver dollar, and Ferguson gave him a quarter. The man tried to twist it against his teeth, and decided it was good.

Ferguson asked him curiously, "Come from far?"

"Far enough," said the man. "Delaware."

"Going far?"

"No farther'n necessary." He started to lead his big dun horse onto the dock.

"If you're stopping here, my name is Ferguson."

The horse's hooves thudded hollowly on the planks as the man swung him around. "Not that it's any of your business," he said with no apparent malice, "but my name is George Keller, scouting the land for Zachariah Mawson."

"I have not had the pleasure," said Ferguson.

"Mawson is two days away with four grown sons and twelve thousand head of sheep, headed for Nebrasky."

"It seems no concern of mine."

"He will want passage for the sheep."

Ferguson hesitated, and looked at the opposite shore and the gray-topped wagons. "I will show him a place to swim them," he said.

"No swimming," said Keller. "The loss is too heavy. Ain't you in business to make money?"

"I'm also in business to ferry emigrants — and yon shore is thick with some who had waited for days." He turned back to Keller. "It would take several days to move that many sheep, and meantime, the emigrants would have to wait."

"Isn't one man's money as good as another's?"

"In the wagons," said Ferguson, "there are women and children."

"I have heard you don't like sheep," said Keller.

"I've nothing against them," said Ferguson, noting the children drawing up in a semi-circle behind Keller. "But my first duty is to people."

"Your first duty is to the man who offers the fare."

"Provided he comes in his proper turn," said Ferguson, watching him.

"How many are ahead?"

Ferguson waved at the Iowa shore. "All those."

Keller asked suddenly, "Have they all applied for passage?"

Ferguson began to get his back up. "By setting their wagons there, they have applied," he said. "Mr. Mawson will have to wait his proper turn — about four days."

Keller sneered. "What's your price?" he demanded.

"Ten cents a head."

Keller snorted. "For sheep? It was four cents over the Mississippi."

"This is not the Mississippi," said Ferguson.

"We will give you six."

"The price is ten."

Keller studied him for a moment. "I will meet you halfway."

Ferguson glanced at the men ashore, listening. He turned back to Keller. "I will meet you halfway between six and ten. The price will be eight — no less."

"It's robbery."

Ferguson took a step toward him, and noticed the great breadth of the man's shoulders. "It is the price," he said quietly.

Keller fixed his black eyes on Ferguson for a moment, and then unexpectedly conceded. "Mr. Mawson won't like it," he said.

"I will have to risk that," said Ferguson.

Speculation was in Keller's eyes as he tried to size up Ferguson. "It may be a bigger gamble than you bargain for."

Ferguson said thoughtfully, "I worked ten years in the coal mines, where every day was a gamble for a man's life, so I don't suppose this one will be anything unfamiliar."

Keller got on his horse and sat him straight-backed — not round-shouldered like a cow-hand. "If you're goin' to wet-nurse emigrants, you better get some sugar-tits on hand, because there's plenty of 'em coming."

"No more than usual, I imagine."

"A *lot* more than usual. All the way from Indiana. There's a panic in the East, and everybody who isn't tied down — and some who are — is leaving."

"Headed for where?" asked Ferguson.

"Anywhere there's free land." The dun shook its head impatiently. "Where's the townsite around here?"

"There isn't any," said Ferguson.

"They're selling lots back East, and they said the townsite was close to Ferguson's Ferry."

"Have you bought a lot?" asked Ferguson.

"What difference does it make?"

"Not much," said Ferguson, beginning to find it hard to feel friendly toward the man. "But I know of no townsite closer than Catherine on the west or Tehama on the south — and they aren't close. Perhaps it is somewhere else in Nebraska."

"I know what they told me," said Keller, seeming sure of himself.

"I got a prospectus here," piped up the little man on the wagon, digging a thick wad of folded paper from inside his shirt.

Ferguson went across the deck to look at it, and he heard the hooves of Keller's horse clomp on the planks behind him as Keller turned his horse to watch.

The little man put his feet up on the edge of the wagon box and began to unfold the map on his legs, while Ferguson walked in close to the wheel to see the map, and Keller, on his horse, drew up to the doubletree. "Was you bothered by Indians?" Keller asked.

The little man looked up. "Miz Hudson and me, we come through a bunch, but they never paid us much mind. My wife was scairt, but I figgered they was only after somethin' to steal."

Keller looked darkly across the river. "An Indian will take a mile for every inch you allow him. We was pestered all the way from the Mississippi."

"These Oto Indians will not harm you," said Ferguson. "They have not been treated too well, and they resent it, but I don't think —"

"What you think," Keller said with unexpected vehemence, "don't amount to a damn when an Indian starts wavin' a scalping knife."

Ferguson looked up at him. "The Otos are friendly," he said quietly.

"They're Indians," Keller said, as if it were a terrible indictment, "and this country ain't safe with them around." He put his hand on the butt of a pistol, hanging from the saddle-horn. "I aim to do my share to make it safe."

Ferguson turned to face him. "Because you want to make it safe, or because you figure that's the quickest way to be a hero without danger to your own hide?"

Keller came down fast. He landed hard on both feet, and as he did, Ferguson lowered his

31

head and waded into him with both arms pumping. He backed him into the dun, which was thrown off balance, staggered against the side of the wagon, and neighed in fright.

Hudson grabbed the reins of his team and began to mutter, "Whoa, now; whoa, boy!"

Keller finally got his feet under him and came back with a rush. Liquor was strong on his breath, and Ferguson gave ground cautiously. Then Keller caught him between the eyes with a hard fist, and Ferguson stumbled backward. Keller hit him again, boring in with the sure instinct of a killer, but Ferguson backed toward the end of the ferry. He shook off the fogginess in his head, and kept Keller at a distance, then he moved back in, throwing long lefts and rights that landed with a crack of bones. Keller backed away and almost fell into the crack between the ferry and the dock, but recovered in time to move backward on the dock, now seeming puzzled at the relentless attack of Ferguson.

Keller charged, but Ferguson sidestepped and whirled. From behind, he seized Keller's jacket as Keller was turning, and spun him. Keller was off-balance, and his feet slammed on the planks as he tried to keep from falling. Ferguson spun him entirely around once, and as Keller came to a stop, Ferguson, poised, hit him three times with each fist, and Keller went down hard.

Ferguson went back on the ferry, led the dun

horse across to the dock, and slapped it hard on the rump with his open hand. The horse bolted off the dock and slowed down, and was caught by Simmons.

Ferguson went back to Hudson. "Let's see that map again," he said, rubbing his hands to limber them. He ached all over — and his side throbbed painfully with each breath.

The little man was staring at him.

"Simon!" cried the fat woman.

Hudson came to with a start. "Yes, Marthy."

"The gentleman asked to see the map."

Hudson brought himself back to reality with an obvious effort. "Yes, sir." He picked up the map from the floor of the wagon and put it again on his legs, and wrapped the reins around the foot-iron. "Now, see here," he said in his Kentucky twang. Here it is. It says 'Logan City' in these here big letters."

"It does, for sure," Ferguson agreed, staring at the highly-colored lithograph of an extensive street plan.

"According to this here," said Hudson, "the townsite is only nine miles from Ferguson's Ferry."

Ferguson shook his head slowly. "There is no townsite that close to the ferry."

"There *has* to be," said Hudson. "It shows it on the map."

"Anybody who can pay for it," said Ferguson, "can have a map printed."

"But it shows streets and all," said Hudson, beginning to sound scared.

"I see it does." Ferguson examined the map more carefully, noting with dismay the neatly drawn streets, the stream marked simply "River," the square marked "City Hall," and others labeled "Fire Department," "First Methodist Church," "Academy of Learning" and "Female Seminary." Finally he looked up at Hudson. "Have you bought a lot from this plat?" he asked.

"Two of 'em, right across from the railway station, there." Hudson pointed with a trembling forefinger. "Do you think there's something wrong?"

Ferguson asked him: "Why did you choose lots close to the railway station?"

"We're goin' to put in a bakery. My wife bakes the best bread in the state of Kentucky, and I can make real good pies. We had a bakery back home, and did real well. But we got all these children." He looked around. "They need some room to grow."

"How much did you pay for these lots?" asked Ferguson.

The little man began to turn pale. "Four hundred apiece. The man said they were worth five, but he let me have them for four."

Ferguson looked at the bold legend across the bottom of the lithographed sheet: *Logan City, Nebraska Territory's Coming Metropolis. (Take the north route to Ferguson's Ferry.)* He looked up finally and said, "Mr. Hudson, you may have lots, but there is no such

34

townsite to my knowledge."

"But the man said —"

"I suppose you wanted to sell bakery goods to travelers."

"We aimed —"

"But I must give you the unpleasant news that there is no railroad in the territory of Nebraska."

The woman spoke up. "Maybe it's building, Simon."

"It may be building," said Ferguson, "but I do not know of it. How much money do you have left?"

"We sold out for twelve hundred," said the little man. "I paid eight hundred for the lots. We bought clothes, and the wagon and team, and I guess we's mighty near broke," he confessed.

"Well, you're strong," said Ferguson, handing him back the map, "and your wife looks strong and your children look healthy. You'll be able to find something."

The little man tried to moisten his lips, but his tongue was dry. "There has to be a Logan City," said Hudson almost in a whisper. "There has to be!"

His wife began to cry silently, and one of the small children started to whimper.

Ferguson said, "There are lots of supplies needed by the emigrants when they get across. It might be you could freight up from Omaha City."

"I don't know what to do with the wife and young 'uns," said Hudson dully, still trying to understand what had developed.

"There's Turner's Tavern up the road a piece — a respectable place, and he might have some work for you."

"Two lots — right across from the railway station." Hudson looked up at Ferguson, suddenly fierce. "Mr. Ferguson, if I ever see that man again, I swear I'll strangle him with my bare hands."

"You won't, likely. Would you like me to lead your team off the ferry?" asked Ferguson.

"No, I can drive 'em off." He picked up the reins while Ferguson went to the back post to pull the ferry up against the dock. The children — ten of them — streamed onto the deck before the team got into action; Mrs. Hudson was holding a baby in her lap by that time, and a small girl peered out from the opening in the canvas. The little man rolled the wagon out on the dock, with boards rattling under the weight of horses' hooves and wagon wheels; then the little man called, "Whoa!" and got down from his seat, clambering awkwardly over the front wheel. "The fare," he said. "I forgot to pay."

Ferguson was on the point of telling him it was free, but thought better of it. "One dollar," he said.

Hudson dug into a grubby clamshell purse. "The man on the other bank said it was two dollars," he said suddenly.

Ferguson noted that the purse was almost empty.

"It's one dollar," he said.

Benson came up as they drove off. Ferguson signaled Teddy Root on the opposite bank and the ferry began to slip back to the east. Keller was leading the dun toward the watching men. No Horse came down the slope with the mules, and Keller stared at him. Ferguson watched, but Keller made no move. No Horse led the mules to the open space around the fire. "It's time for their corn," he said.

Ferguson nodded, and No Horse went to the sack and dipped into it with both hands to fill a corral.

"Why di'n't you let Hudson go for nothin'?" asked Benson. "You've done it before."

Ferguson watched Hudson's horses go into the pull as the wagon started up the incline to the slope. "That man is in a fair way to go to pieces," he observed. "He needs something to save his pride."

"You know what that map means?"

Ferguson looked sharply at him. "It means the promoters are about to move in," he said.

CHAPTER III

WHILE THE FERRY was moving back across the river, Ferguson climbed the short slope to the level prairie where Benson had unhooked his mules and was bringing them back to the starting point.

"You collect the fares for a while," said Ferguson, looking at Benson. "But, mind you, no fighting." He looked absently at the leather-faced little man whose scraggly beard was beginning to turn gray. "It is possible," Ferguson said, "that they will send over more strong-arm men to wear me down."

"Who?"

Ferguson shook his head. "I don't know — but these repeated disputes are no accidents. They are done to wear me down."

"Two fights before breakfast *is* overdoin' it, I'd say."

Ferguson eyed him for a moment. "Remember what I said. If you get into an argument, tell them to come back later when I'll be here."

"I ain't afraid of them," said Benson, "but you're the boss."

Ferguson started up the slope, but Logan met him, his pointed black beard giving him a peculiarly satanic look.

"You're a scrapper, Ferguson. You proved it. Now stop this constant fighting and join our forces. There is a lot of money to be made here, and we can make it easier if you will quit standing in the way."

Ferguson looked him over. "I'm not sure I know exactly what you're driving at," he said.

Logan gave a snort of impatience. "You're either awful dumb or real smart," he said.

"Call it anything you like."

"Look, Ferguson. The ferry is the key to the country. You can, to start with, hold people up on the other side until they will agree to buy lots from us. You can let those cross first and let them cross cheap, while you hold the others back."

"It doesn't seem exactly fair," said Ferguson.

"It's business."

"That doesn't make it right."

"We could separate those with money from those without money, and pick out the ones with money for this area. You could quit sympathizing with those who have bought lots — send them on west to Kearny or some place. Ferguson, I tell you, there's a gold mine here if you play it right."

"I am not much of a promoter," said Ferguson.

"You don't have to promote. Come in with us, and we'll see you're taken care of."

"Who's 'we'?"

"Yeakel and me — maybe one or two others."

"Simmons?"

"He is only a hanger-on; he does odd jobs," said Logan.

"Like taking Mr. Benson's quarter?"

"He did that on his own hook."

"Is Wiggins in with you?" asked Ferguson.

"Never saw the man before."

"How about Keller?" asked Ferguson.

He saw a reservation in Logan's dark eyes, and the man said, "I've heard of him."

Ferguson said quietly, "You don't really expect me to help you, do you?"

"Every man has a price," said Logan.

"It may be," said Ferguson, "but I will have to think on mine."

He walked a quarter of a mile to the north, where his sorrel saddle horse was staked in a draw, and saddled and rode out to the west. The broad trail of emigrant wagons and stock led first to Turner's Tavern.

Ferguson saw the older Turner girl go out back with a water-pail, and he turned the sorrel toward the dug well. The girl had snapped the wooden bucket onto the end of the rope and was lowering it, when she heard Ferguson's horse and looked around.

"Good morning, Miss Sally," he said.

Ferguson dismounted. She began to smile — almost shyly, he noticed for the first time. Did that mean she was growing up? He looked more closely at her, and realized that she had already grown up, that she was, in fact, crowding her thin dress in two places.

He had better remember to tell Tom that she ought to start wearing something under the dress. Sally did not know about things like that, for the Turners had started west when she was little; her mother had died, and Ferguson guessed that Sally had never had a chance to talk to another woman until Tom had settled there and opened the tavern. He smiled at her. "You have boarders this morning?"

She nodded, her eyes on his for a moment. "Some of them folks from Ohio. One wagon stopped last night; the other'ne come by a little while ago."

He reached for the rope and she put her shoulder in the way of his arm while she jerked the rope a couple of times to tip the bucket, then watched the rope start through her fingers as the bucket filled and began to sink. Then she turned toward him and put the rope in his hands. He began the long pull, hand over hand, while she seated herself lightly on a kerosene barrel and swung her legs, hitting her bare heels against the barrel.

"Why do you watch me so closely?" he asked.

She smiled. "I jist enjoy seein' you work — you move so smooth."

"Sally," he said, "you're getting grown-up."

She said, tossing her head, "I'll be sixteen next week."

He reached down and lifted the bucket out and set it by the coil of rope. She left the top of the barrel and dropped lightly to her feet.

She changed the bucket to the other hand. "You comin' in, Mr. Ferguson?"

"No, thanks. I have to get on to feed my stock."

"Pa made some mighty good pancakes this mornin'."

He grinned at her. "You almost talked me into it," he said. "I'll stop on the way back. I want to see how Noah is coming along with the well."

"He said last night he was down to a hundred and ninety-six feet."

He nodded. "No sign of water yet, though. How deep is your well?"

"Almost three hundred, pa said."

"I'll have a ways to go, I guess."

She pushed the door in a little. "If you don't take too long I'll see there's pancakes left for you, Mr. Ferguson."

He moistened his lips and said, "I'll be back after a while, Miss Sally."

"You're sure in an all-fired hurry for that well, Mr. Ferguson."

"Just because I have to spend so much time hauling water from the river. The time to be in a real hurry," he said, "will be when it starts to show water. Then we'll have to get down there fast and start digging in the right direction."

"Whyn't you take your time?" she asked.

"Because a little digging might open the sand and get a nice flow — but if you fool around, pretty soon the bottom of the well will be under water, and you'll never have another chance."

It was two miles to his half section, and Tom Turner's corn was a foot high: even without rain for three weeks, it would be knee-high by the Fourth of July. Ferguson's own corn had gone in a week later, but was not far behind. It was rich soil, but nobody knew as yet whether the rain would come at the right time.

His cabin, of logs skidded in from the river, was as large as he could make it from the timber available. Out in front were a freight wagon with the tongue propped up on a stump, and a wedge-shaped lizard that held three kerosene barrels for hauling water. He had put the well on the far side of the house, between the cabin and a one-walled barn. They were digging a four-foot hole, and if a man wanted to be safe, he would shore about every three feet down until he hit water. He lowered the boards, already sawed to length, and toenailed them into one another or sometimes nailed a two-by-two in the corner if he wanted to be sure; it depended on the character of the earth.

He rode alongside the stone curbing he had put up to hold the windlass, and leaned over. For a moment he could see nothing; then Noah Turner's voice echoed up to him, reverberating hollowly from one side of the well to the other: "That you, Mr. Ferguson?"

"It's me," said Ferguson. "You got a lot of dirt to take out?"

"A fair amount. It's gittin' too thick down here to dig."

"Fill the tub and I'll get the mule."

He rode off to the west where the mule and the two oxen were lying in the shade of a big, wild-plum bush. They slanted the shoring out from the center at the bottom of every section, so they could raise a tubful of dirt without obstruction, but at two hundred feet, the job of raising the dirt called for a mule or an ox. The animals had grazed early and were sleepy, and he walked up to the mule and got it by the halter, and tied his hair-rope to the halter and trotted back, leading the mule. He put a collar and trace-chains on the mule, and a singletree, and looped the rope through the clevis. "All ready?" he called down the hole.

Presently Noah's voice floated back eerily: "Go ahead."

Ferguson got the mule started, and knew it would continue until he called, "Whoa!" He went back to the well. "All right down there?"

"Fine," said Noah.

Presently Ferguson could see the tub below, and he went out to the mule, got it by the halter, and waited for the flag on the rope. When he saw it, he stopped the mule and left it leaning into the collar while he went back to lift the tub over the side and dump it; he would spread the dirt later with a drag. Then he lowered the tub back into the hole, and went to turn the mule toward the well.

He took out four loads, and he guessed that Noah had been down as far as he could go; he lowered planks and nails, and then Noah came up for a breather. He was a small boy, a year younger than Sally, and dressed in nothing but overalls, which now were soaked with the good smell of fresh earth. He brushed the dirt from his overalls, and Ferguson said, "You better take 'em off and shake 'em."

"Ready to go for breakfast?" asked Ferguson. "I'll ride you double."

"I got a lunch," said Noah. "Pa killed a couple of wild turkeys day before yesterday, and Sally made me some sandwiches."

"Take your time eating. Then I'll let you down again. Get lonesome down there?"

"Sometimes it's scary," said Noah. "It's dark when you first go down — but after a while you get used to it and you can see pretty good. Only thing, the sky is sure a long way off."

Ferguson had observed the boy's work, and knew that he put up shoring as well as any man. "Don't take any chances with those planks," he said, "and be sure the rope is always where you can reach it."

"I ain't worried, Mr. Ferguson."

They kept a strong stick firmly tied crosswise at the end of the three-hundred-and-forty-foot rope, and if a man should be inadvertently left alone, he could get out with the help of the

45

rope by taking advantage of the toeholds in the shoring. It wasn't very risky, for they were doing it all over the territory, and nobody had been lost in a well yet.

Noah came back wiping his mouth on the back of his forearm. "Guess I'm good till noon, Mr. Ferguson."

Ferguson held the rope while Noah got into the tub, then let it down, hand over hand. The mule felt the pull and began to back up, following the rope in to the well. Presently the rope stopped going down, and Noah's voice floated up: "All right, Mr. Ferguson."

He unfastened the rope from the mule's collar, examined the big knot some eight feet from the end, and made sure the stick was firmly tied crosswise. He threw a double half-hitch around the log upright, and called down: "So long."

He heard the sound of a pick in hard dirt, and then Noah's weird voice: "So long, Mr. Ferguson."

He mounted the sorrel and turned back to the east, but struck out across the prairie to the north of east, toward a cabin that sat alone in the middle of a claim. A fire burned under an iron pot in the yard and as Ferguson drew near, a woman came from the cabin with a bucket of water. She lifted the bucket with an effort and poured the water into a V-shaped hopper, from which it drained into another bucket at the bottom.

Ferguson dismounted. "Mrs. Talbot, can I help you?" he asked.

"I have been taking care of my own work," she said, and a calculating but otherwise inscrutable expression came into her black eyes. "Whether you can really help me," she said, "I don't know, and I am not sure I will ever find out."

He knew what she meant, and recognized it also as a challenge that stirred him in spite of its unexpectedness. He moved a step toward her, but said only: "I am sorry that trouble arose with your brother-in-law."

She said something he had not anticipated: "Wiggins is a man of no sense at all."

"It may be," he said, "that he did not act for himself."

She moved to the pot and stirred the boiling fat with a bleached broom handle. Then she took an egg from her apron pocket and dropped it in the leaching water, watched it sink slowly, and fished it out with a big spoon.

He said, "What are you going to do with your homestead, Mrs. Talbot? You can't very well farm it by yourself."

"What else can I do?"

"What do you want to do?" he asked.

She turned to him with unexpected fire in her eyes. "I want to get out of this God-forsaken country — where there are no shoes, no men who aren't married, no rain, and —"

"Tom Turner isn't married," he pointed out.

Her eyes flashed scorn. "He's too fat to need a woman."

He tried to avoid the obvious answer. "People come into the territory every day."

But she did not fall into his scheme to keep the discussion away from himself. She moved toward him. "And you, Mr. Ferguson, are thin enough, but I doubt you would know what to do with a woman if you had one."

He knew she was goading him, and he was aware that she was a beautiful woman except for that trace of hardness.

He said, "It is a fair country, with the biggest sky I have ever seen."

He sensed her disappointment, and she turned away.

"You own the ferry," she said. "You are in a place to become the wealthiest and most powerful man in this part of the country."

"I don't see how."

"You know every person who comes into this part of Nebraska. You can sell them land, insurance, goods — anything they want. Or, you can keep them out if you want."

"I don't try to keep anybody out," he said. "I carry anybody who waits his turn and pays his fare."

She moved a step closer to him. "You *could* keep out the wrong people," she said.

"Perhaps I could — but I won't."

"There is more money to be made from people than from tilling this sun-baked soil," she said.

"But not the satisfaction."

"Satisfaction means different things to different people." She set the bucket back under the leaching-hopper. "I have made fresh coffee this morning," she said, her black eyes again inscrutable. "You are welcome to come in for a while."

"I have to get back," he said.

"You have worked every day since I have been here," she said. "Are you so important that you cannot take a few minutes for a neighborly visit?"

He smiled wryly. "From the way things went this morning, I'm afraid not. But the fact is that I have a number of things to do."

"And perhaps," she said acidulously, "you are more attracted to a barefoot girl with yellow hair than to a grown woman who knows her own mind."

He looked at her for a moment. He did not understand why she referred to Sally, for he and Sally had barely spoken to each other. Finally he said, "I am sorry, Mrs. Talbot." He put his foot in the stirrup. "I suppose I am a man who does not like to be pushed."

"I would suppose," she said emphatically, "that you are a man who will *have* to be pushed — if you are a man."

CHAPTER IV

FERGUSON TIED HIS horse to the hitching-rail. The door was open, and he stooped to go through without bumping his head.

The tavern was a two-room log cabin, with an attic where the family slept. The main room had tables to eat on and chairs and stumps to sit on, and the floor was hard-packed dirt. Oiled deerskin let in light at the window openings, and a two-section hayburner stove sat in the middle of the room, with a stovepipe going to the ceiling. A ladder in one corner led to the attic, and a door on the right led to the second room, where travelers could sleep on a buffalo robe on the floor for fifty cents, or in a corded bed with a corn-shuck mattress for seventy-five.

Tom Turner, who weighed about four hundred — most of it stomach — said, "Howdy, Sandy John."

"Morning, Tom. All your boarders gone?"

"All gone. I hear you had trouble this mornin' at the ferry."

Ferguson nodded.

"Looks like they're tryin' to run you out."

"Maybe."

"Hate to see somebody else run that ferry," said Turner. "The wrong man could cause us a lot of worry."

"I'm still running it," said Ferguson, and looked at Turner. "When I came out here, there was no ferry and there was no land preempted around here at all. I picked out the spot for the ferry and I hewed the wood and built the raft — and I've built everything that goes with it, and I don't think I'd ever sell it at any price. Likewise, I'd fight my hardest to keep anybody from taking it in any other fashion."

Turner nodded slowly. "I didn't know it meant that much to you."

"You got any pancakes left?" asked Ferguson.

Turner called: "Sally!"

She appeared at once in the door from the lean-to, where the cooking was done. "Yes, pa."

"Mr. Ferguson wants somethin' to eat."

Ferguson turned to Turner, "Have you given any thought to a claim club?"

"Considerable," said Turner. "Don't see how we're gonna put it off any longer. Got any ideas?"

"Several." Ferguson sat down as Sally brought in a glass of water. "The thing that hits me first is that my place is my place. I didn't take it away from anybody else. Nobody had settled on it until I came along and built a cabin, but now the scalawags come in, and they think I have a fortune, and they see the ferry as a means of controlling lands and people. But I don't see it that way. The ferry can be used to help, and was not meant to control." He drained the glass of water. "The first thing to

51

do is get together a sizeable group of men who want to keep the land they already have."

"That hadn't ought to be hard," said Turner. "There's three or four comin' now." He pointed toward the open door, beyond which a number of men had ridden up on horseback; they went to the rail and dismounted, talking heatedly.

"Nobody's goin' to take my claim," said one, "if I have to fight 'em off with a shotgun."

They came in, stooping to go through the low doorway. "Got any beer, Tom?"

Turner waddled to the corner, got four big tin cups, and filled them from a barrel that stood on end on a cracker hogshead.

"Good scraps you put up this morning," said Nosey Porter.

"Too good," said Ferguson. "I feel like a wrung-out pair of stockings."

"A man can't keep it up forever," said Roy Ernest, a very tall man with double-jointed ankles. "What are we going to do?"

Black Gallagher, a beetle-browed Irishman, offered his opinion: "Faith, and a half dozen men with shillelaghs would make believers out of them."

Turner said, "It might lead to gun-play, and some of us might get killed."

Sally came in with the pancakes, a steaming plateful, six high, with honey and butter.

Hans Osterman, a light-haired German, slammed the table with his open hand. "Now there's a man has got some sense."

Sally stood by the table, and Ferguson said, "You have coffee?"

"Sandy John was sayin' it's time to organize a claim club," said Turner.

Roy Ernest looked up quizzically. "What's a claim club?" he asked.

Osterman called to Sally: "*Fraulein,* you got more of them *pfannkuchen?* I ain't had 'em since my old lady died of the consumption."

Sally turned in the doorway to the lean-to. "I will bring you some," she said.

Ferguson talked between bites. "A claim club is unofficial," he said, "but when the scalawags try to take everything, it's the only protection we have."

Gallagher asked bluntly, "You think they're tryin' to take everything, or just your ferry?"

Ferguson looked up. "Not just the ferry," he said. "It's the best cash crop in the territory right now, but it won't last, and it's not worth getting in trouble over."

"Then why?" asked Ernest.

"To control this part of the country. By refusing passage, a man could keep some people out — or he could raise the fares to some. Likewise, he could steer the newcomers to his friends." He watched Sally set down the coffee. "There are many ways in which the ferry could be used to fill a man's pocketbook or to keep a group of men in control."

There was the sound of horses outside.

53

"*You* ain't played favorites," Gallagher observed.

Ferguson grinned wryly. "Too independent, I guess. I don't like to get in a position where somebody else can tell me what to do."

A big man appeared at the doorway, his large frame caused him to stoop far down to enter. He was Dave Ackerman, from near the store called Chippewa — where Logan published the *Chronicle*.

"Howdy, gents," Ackerman's big, booming voice filled the room, but there were no echoes in those log cabins.

"Come in and sit a while," said Turner. "We was just talkin' about the high price of goobers."

Roy Ernest untangled his long legs. "How are things in your neck of the woods?"

Half a dozen men filed in behind Ackerman and spread around the room.

"We heard you was having a meeting," said Ackerman. "Mind if we set in?"

Ferguson smiled. "News sure gets around. It didn't start till half an hour ago. Maybe you just figured it was time for a meeting," he suggested.

"Beer, gents?" asked Turner.

"Sure," said Ackerman. "Beer for ev'rybody."

Tom turned to the pile of tin cups.

"I was at the ferry this mornin'," said Ackerman, "and I seen what happened. It looks like there's no question but the highbinders are tryin' to get control."

"It does have the look of a campaign," said Ferguson.

"I heard about the sheep," said Ackerman, sitting down. "Is that calc'lated to make things hard for you?"

Ferguson shrugged. "It could be honest enough, but the fact is it will tie up the ferry for three or four days, depending on how the sheep take to it."

"Meantime," said Gallagher, "them on the other side will be faunchin'."

"And cussin' you," said Osterman, "and sendin' committees to wait on you."

Ferguson sighed. "Worst of all, I will have to take the sheep out of turn."

"I'm damned if I would!" said Ackerman.

Sally came in with a plate of pancakes for Osterman.

"I'll take some of them," said Ackerman.

She smiled at him. "I'll put some on, Mr. Ackerman."

Ernest asked, "Is there any place lower down, where they could build a ferry?"

"If they have found such a place," said Ferguson, "it will be dangerous — for I was up and down the river in a boat for several days. The Missouri is tricky, and full of strange currents and sand bars and caving banks. I don't think there is another safe place for twenty miles on either side."

"Some people don't worry about things bein' safe," said Turner, bringing beer.

"We were talking about forming a claim club," said Ferguson.

Ackerman looked up quickly from his beer. "Ain't that vigilantes?"

Ferguson said, "In a way."

"Whyn't we get a sheriff out here?" asked Ernest.

"To do what?"

"To keep these fellers from takin' our land."

Ferguson finished his pancake. "A sheriff would have no law to enforce, because you don't own the land legally."

"They're goin' to throw the land open for settlement."

"But they haven't yet," said Ferguson, "and we need something to bridge the gap until the settlement laws come into effect."

"We *were* a mite early," Ernest admitted.

"We all took property under the pre-emption law, and while it is not illegal, still we have no legal basis for a title until the land is surveyed and a government land office established, so we can register our claims. In the meantime, the brigands and newcomers are free to jump our claims unless we are strong enough to keep them off."

One of Ackerman's friends said, "You mean *fight*, with *rifles*?"

Ferguson looked at him with understanding, for Job Sye was a small man, thin-haired, past the age to be fighting. "Some kind of force is all that stands between us and losing our land," said Ferguson kindly.

"Somebody will get killed," Sye said fearfully. "And I've got an ailing wife and nine children."

"I think," said Ferguson, "that if we can organize, to let the scoundrels know that we stand together, there will be less chance that anybody will get killed, and we are not likely to lose our land before the law comes."

"How long do you figure that will be?" asked Osterman.

"Maybe a year, maybe two — maybe only a few weeks."

"Why don't we wait?" said Sye. "We could always swear that we settled here first."

"The man who is on the land when the survey comes in, is the man who will get his claim recorded."

There was silence, and in that silence Sally Turner came in with the pancakes for Ackerman, and the silence continued until she had gone back into the kitchen. Then Ackerman cleared his throat. "How do we take the first step?" he asked.

"Post a public notice of a meeting to organize a claim club, which will assume authority to settle all claims in the Blackbird Creek area."

"Why post a notice?" asked Gallagher. "Whyn't we organize right here and now, before they find out what's goin' on?"

"That's not the best way," said Tom Turner. "The best way is to make it public, so nobody can claim they was left out."

"What next?" asked Ackerman, pouring honey on his pancakes.

"We meet, elect temporary officers, adopt a constitution and bylaws, then elect permanent officers. We will select a jury to decide all claims. We know who is here now, and we won't let anybody take over."

"What if they do?" asked Sye. "What if somebody like Keller comes up some day with a six-shooter and orders me and my folks off the land?"

"Do as you are told. Then go to the officers of the claim club. They will pick a jury and have a trial, and if the man on trial has shoved you off the land, the jury will decide against him."

But Sye persisted. "What if he don't pay any attention to the jury?"

"The president of the claim club appoints a committee to wait on him. He might, for instance, be ducked in the river until he sees the light."

"He might hold 'em off with a rifle," said Ackerman.

"In such a case," said Ferguson, "the claim club will have to be ready to fight back with rifles."

Sally came in with coffee, and nobody spoke for a moment. Then Ernest said, "What's to keep the scalawags from organizin' themselves?"

"Nothing," Ferguson said, "except the knowledge that they are in the wrong. They

58

might organize anyway," he added, "but organizing like that never seems to work too well against people who are organized in the right."

Ackerman slammed the table with his fist. "I say let's organize. Otherwise, I know what's going to happen. I was at the ferry this morning, and I saw what they are up to. Wiggins and Keller both started a ruckus, and Simmons and Yeakel and Charlie Logan stood there like humps on a log, and never raised a finger. They was hopin' you would be licked."

"I know," said Ferguson. "They don't want anybody in this part of the country who might speak out against them."

"We'll organize, then. When do we have the meeting?"

"Tonight!" said Osterman loudly.

"That's too soon. We'll post a notice today at the ferry, for a meeting tomorrow night at the tavern. That will give everybody plenty of time to hear about it."

"You want me to write out a notice?" asked Ferguson.

"Sure," said Ackerman. "Write out a notice for seven o'clock tomorrow night, and we'll all be here with bells on."

Ferguson got up and paid Turner for his meal. "I'm going to see Yeakel and Logan," he said, "and try to find out if they are close to Simmons, and exactly who is behind it."

CHAPTER V

IT WAS A long, hot ride to the Chippewa post office, and Ferguson had a couple of hours to think things over. He followed the rutted trail into Chippewa City — one house and two store-buildings. Simmons owned the general store and lived upstairs. The *Chronicle* occupied the second building, and Charlie Logan had a room in the back. Yeakel's office was on one side at the front, while the post office, run by Logan, was on the other side, and opened directly into the printing office.

Ferguson tied his horse in front of the post office, and walked through the dust to the front door, where a gold-lettered sign said, *United States Post Office. Charles Logan, P.M.* He went inside. The right-hand door was open, and Yeakel stood with his back to the door while he looked through a pile of quarter-folded newspapers that teetered precariously on top of the desk. Ferguson went to the barred window, but saw nobody. The fresh smell of linseed oil and varnish, and the cool smell of paper indicated that Logan was around, however, and Ferguson went to the middle door and stepped inside. At the back of the shop, past the type-cases and the G. Wash handpress, Logan was working on an imposing-stone with cans and a wooden mixing-stick. His arms were smeared with black almost to the elbows, but his shirt sleeves had been rolled up high.

Ferguson said, "Logan, I think you went overboard on that plat. You need two sections for a townsite, but you and Yeakel together haven't anything near that, to say nothing of a railroad."

Logan shrugged. "It's not entirely imaginative, as you seem to imply. Such a town will be built as soon as we sell enough lots."

"On whose land?"

Logan raised his eyebrows. "Who knows? Men are going broke every day. Some of them will sell out cheap."

"One thing I don't understand," said Ferguson thoughtfully. "Why did you ever put your name on that plat?"

An unexpected change came over Logan's face. He said softly, "Didn't you ever want to leave something behind that you could be remembered by?"

"I guess I never thought about it," said Ferguson, a little startled, for he had not suspected such a sentiment in the editor.

Logan changed back quickly. "Have you made up your mind to work with us instead of against us?" asked Logan.

"I like to know those who are working with me," said Ferguson. "I don't think that you and Yeakel are in this alone. Simmons is a little man, grabbing what he can from the leavings. He and Wiggins and Keller are all hired men —

but somewhere there is a bigger man, and I'd like to know who he is before I give my answer."

Logan said quietly, "You're asking a lot of information."

"There must be answers."

"I suppose there are," said Logan, "but I have to get on with my ink-making for tomorrow's paper."

"I want to put a notice in," said Ferguson.

"All right. You got it written out?"

"No."

"I'll write it for you." He started wiping his hands on an old shirt, and finished by pouring kerosene over his hands and wiping them again. Then he took a pencil and went to a stack of huge white sheets, and said, "All right."

" 'Notice to the public'," Ferguson began. " 'On Friday evening, June 24, 1859, at Turner's Tavern, interested residents of the countryside will meet to discuss formation of a claim club to sustain pre-emption rights until a U.S. Land Office can be established in this neighborhood'."

Logan stared at him. "You mean it, Ferguson?"

"Certainly I mean it. Why not?"

Logan paused. "That's kind of a radical step, isn't it?"

"Wouldn't you say something radical needed to be done, after what happened this morning?"

"What happened out of the way?"

Ferguson restrained his impatience. "For three days now, there has been at least one fight a day at the ferry. You stood there and watched two of them this morning, and you never lifted a finger. Don't you see anything out of the way in that?"

"Well," said Logan, "these people get tired of waiting. Some have to stay over there for a week."

"Nobody stays for a week unless he wants to. The trouble does not come from honest emigrants anyway."

"From where, then?"

"From people put up to it by others who want to make trouble."

"I hope you're not insinuating —"

Ferguson smiled. "If the shoe fits you, Mr. Logan —"

"Why would I have an interest in the ferry?"

"I didn't say you did, Mr. Logan. You could have, though, if you thought it would interfere with your printing of all the copies that go back East to seduce emigrants to Nebraska Territory."

Logan's beard moved rapidly for a moment as he moved his chew to the other side of his mouth. "There is nothing wrong about that, Ferguson. I merely print the papers and sell them to the Emigrant Aid Society."

Ferguson picked up a quarter-folded paper. "Then this story must have come from somewhere else." He read aloud: " 'A farmer from up near Ferguson's Ferry was in today with his first vegetables of the season: a cucumber that measured eighteen and a half inches from end to end, and a potato that weighed fourteen pounds. He tells us that the corn up there will make at least ninety bushels per acre. It is already knee-high, and gets plenty of sunshine and has had lots of rain. Veritably, this is the garden-spot of America.' "

Logan's eyes narrowed. "What about it?"

"There has never been a crop raised up there because nobody has been there long enough. There has been no rain since the first of May; it is too early for cucumbers and potatoes, and nobody in the territory will make ninety bushels of corn to the acre."

Ferguson heard Major Yeakel cross the hall to the printing office door, and stop.

"The readers expect some exaggeration," said Logan. "Every paper in the country does it."

"They do it — but do the readers know they are doing it?"

Yeakel said from behind him: "It is traditional to put on your best face, Mr. Ferguson."

Ferguson turned. "Is it traditional also to lie?"

"I hardly call this a lie," Yeakel said smoothly.

"I do," said Ferguson. "You are trying to attract emigrants here so you can make loans to them at prohibitive rates." He looked at Yeakel,

64

a very thin man with brown muttonchops. "What are you going to do when these farmers can't pay their loans?"

Yeakel raised his eyebrows. "It doesn't matter. I get my commission when I make the loan."

"And if a man does not make a crop this year, he loses his claim along with his house as well and whatever improvements he has made."

Yeakel shrugged. "It's risky for both sides."

"Of course. If the farmer goes broke, his property will not begin to pay the loan."

"That's for the loan company to worry about," Yeakel said steadily.

Ferguson controlled his impatience. "Aren't you concerned with what happens to the men — to the country?"

Yeakel stared at him. "I'm a businessman," he said. "I am here to make money."

"At the expense of ruination?"

"That is not my responsibility. I am not a wet-nurse for a thousand families of simpleton farmers. I came out here to make money, and I certainly would not live in this Godforsaken country for any other reason."

Ferguson thought about it for a moment, then turned back to Logan. "You got it down?"

Logan said slowly, "How do you want it signed?"

" 'John Ferguson.' "

"That will cost you fifty cents," said Logan,

counting the lines with his pencil.

Ferguson said, "I'll not pay you a penny for running that notice."

Logan seemed surprised. "That's actually very cheap. You don't object to paying a fair price for it, do you?"

"That announcement is news," said Ferguson, "and as such you are in the custom of running it for nothing."

"But —"

"But this is something that neither you nor Major Yeakel wants done, so you are going to charge fifty cents for the notice." He looked around at Yeakel, and then back at Logan. "It's news," he said, reassuring himself. "If you don't run it, no matter. I will post a notice at the general store, and I will post another at the ferry. There will be many men at the meeting, Mr. Logan, and if you stay away, the loss will be your own."

"It won't be legal."

"No public meeting has to be published in a newspaper to be legal," Ferguson said, "I am sorry I caused you to waste such a big sheet of paper, Mr. Logan," and turned on his heel and started to walk out.

"By the way," said Logan.

Ferguson stopped and turned around.

"That no-good Indian working for you — you'd better get rid of him."

Ferguson stared at him. "No Horse is a good worker — and bothers nobody."

"He bothers me and he bothers others," said Logan. "Get rid of him or you'll be sorry."

After a moment, Ferguson went past Yeakel, who eyed him coldly, and crossed the street and went into a long, narrow room that smelled of kerosene and whisky and stock tonic.

Mr. Weinstein was a small man, thin, triangular-faced. He wore a neat, gray beard and spoke in a gentle voice: "You want something, Mr. Ferguson?"

"I'd like to post a notice on your bulletin board."

"Certainly. Help yourself. It's open to all."

"It is a notice for the organization of a claim club, Mr. Weinstein. It might cause trouble."

Weinstein looked at him for a moment and then said: "No trouble for me, Mr. Ferguson. Trouble for you, perhaps."

"No more trouble than I have now."

"That is something only you can say, Mr. Ferguson." He got a flat piece of brown paper from under the counter, and handed Ferguson a pencil from behind his ear.

"Write it out, Mr. Ferguson, if you are not afraid to sign it."

Ferguson smiled to himself as he wrote out the notice. He signed it with a flourish, handed it to Weinstein, and asked: "That big enough to suit you, Mr. Weinstein?"

Weinstein smiled gently. "It may not suit everybody, but I suppose you know that."

"If it did suit everybody," said Ferguson, "it would not have to be done."

Weinstein nodded but said nothing.

"Could you let me have an extra piece of paper?"

Weinstein gave one to him.

"Ever hear of a townsite called Logan City?" asked Ferguson.

Weinstein shook his head.

"Do you know how much land Charlie Logan has?"

"A hundred and sixty, I hear."

"And Major Yeakel the same?"

"That's what I hear."

"It isn't much," said Ferguson as he left.

He was leaving Chippewa to go northeast to the ferry when he saw ten or twelve trotting horses moving fairly fast.

Some time before he met them, he knew they were Indians; they did not ride either abreast or in single file like whites, but scattered and in disorder. They reached the trail before he did, and turned toward him.

Ferguson rode up and said, "Howdy."

A bareheaded Indian with black braids and wearing moccasins and shapeless wool trousers said, "Howdy, Sandy John."

Ferguson rode to a stop, and sat sidewise in the saddle to rest. "What are the Otos doing over here?"

Walking Bird said, "We come to pick out our land."

"Land!"

"Washington says we can have land west

of river for reservation."

Ferguson stared at him. "You're sure?"

"Indian agent, Mr. Newcomb, told us."

"It must have been specified land, though."

Walking Bird shrugged. "I don't know what kind of land that is. Mr. Newcomb said it is just south of your farm."

Ferguson frowned. "You don't mean you're just planning to move in today?"

Two of the Indians behind him grunted, but Walking Bird shook his head at them. "We have to wait until Washington moves the whites who have pre-empt' our land."

"That sounds like trouble," said Ferguson.

Walking Bird raised his eyebrows. "Trouble all around. White men coming into our land on the other side, before we get moved. Indian Department says no, you can't do it, but whites do it anyway." He looked sourly at Ferguson. "You must not have a very good chief in Washington."

"Did Newcomb say how soon you could move?"

"He say pretty soon; not many whites on land along river, he thought."

"Let me give you some advice," said Ferguson.

"Sandy John always friend, open his heart to Otos."

"Then listen with care: don't go any closer to white men than you have to, and don't get into any arguments."

Walking Bird smiled. "You think white men won't like it?"

"I know they won't — and you do too."

"White men don't like anything, I guess, but more land."

"Some do."

"If we have one like that in the Oto tribe, we get rid of him — send him to the Sioux."

Ferguson smiled. "Sometimes I wish it could be that simple for us."

"It's very simple: you have a bad man; you punish him, get rid of him."

"You would be safer on the other side of the river," said Ferguson.

"No good. Whites moving in."

"The Indian agent is over there."

Walking Bird said, "I never hurt anybody who behaved himself. I will not hurt white man who minds his own business."

"They don't all mind their own business, though."

"Is their bad luck. Otos great fighters."

"The whites come here with wives and children," said Ferguson. "They have sold out everything, and they come out, and they get scared. If they don't find free land, they won't have anything."

"Not very smart," said Walking Bird. "I have four wives and nine papooses, and I have been moved by Washington three times. They don't ask, they don't tell me I can have any land at all." His bronze arm swept the country to the east. "All this land was Oto land." He turned in his saddle, which was hardly more than a leather pad on a framework of sticks, and gestured to the west. "All this was Oto country. And to the north, and to the south. And now we have none of our own. The soldiers move us. Now the Indian Department says we will have a hundred and sixty acres apiece, where once we had a hundred and sixty sections. And we are supposed to be glad. We have to be glad, for if Washington does not say it, we have nothing at all. White men want what we have now in Iowa. What's the matter with white men? They don't need land. They don't hunt, they don't fight each other. They want land to raise more corn than they can eat. Why does Washington let them do that?"

Ferguson nodded slowly. "We do strange things," he agreed. He looked over the Indians — all young, all somewhat resentful. "Stay out of trouble," he said. "There are men who would like nothing better than to kill some Indians so they can go home and brag."

"Sure," Walking Bird said scornfully. "Maybe we lift some scalps ourselves."

"If you got into a fight, the whole country would go after you, and you could not possibly win in the long run." He smiled. "Your four wives and nine children will eat better if you stay alive."

There was grumbling in the ranks, but Walking Bird quieted them. "We will stay out

71

of trouble," he said. "We just want to look at our land and see what it is like."

"So long." Ferguson rode off, worried far more than he had admitted to the Otos. With violence beginning to run loose in the country, it was bound to hit the Indians if they were anywhere around. A man like Keller would have no compunction.

His mule team was grazing quietly on the flat; Ferguson stopped at the top of the slope and looked down on a group of men arguing with Mr. Benson. The ferry was on the other side, and below him, just off the ferry, were two covered wagons with ox teams, numerous dogs and a large number of children. Ferguson saw Mr. Benson shaking his finger in Charlie Logan's face, and spurred the sorrel into a downhill lope; Logan must have lit out for the ferry while Ferguson was in Weinstein's store. They turned to look as he rode up and swung off the horse, and Ferguson asked, "What's the trouble, Mr. Benson?"

Mr. Benson's voice was trembling when he said: "Him and Major Yeakel and Mr. Simmons and Mr. Wiggins demanded passage to the other side free, but I told them they would have to pay."

Ferguson turned scornfully to them. "If you wanted to start trouble, you could have waited for me."

Major Yeakel said: "We have business on the other side, and we cannot afford to hang around waiting for you."

"Business of organizing trouble for the ferry?" Ferguson demanded.

"Land business," said Logan.

"Perhaps you want to sell more lots in Logan City?"

Simmons spoke up: "What we have in mind is none of your lookout."

"Then why didn't you pay your fare like anybody else?"

"We would have," said Logan, "but your man here got bossy with us."

Ferguson said: "Mr. Benson never gets bossy with anybody. He does the job I pay him to do — and I take it ill that you descended on him all at once. You spoke to me at Chippewa, and you must have hurried here to the ferry as soon as I left, merely to make trouble."

"A very bold indictment," said Major Yeakel.

"A justifiable one," Ferguson answered. "Now what do you want?"

Dave Ackerman and Roy Ernest rode down the slope — Ackerman big on a buckskin horse, Ernest with flapping knees akimbo on a black. Wiggins, his arm in a sling, looked up at the two men calculatingly, then moved a little behind the others and stayed quiet. Simmons said, "We want across, but we don't see no —"

"Perhaps," said Major Yeakel, "we do not want to cross on your ferry, after your inhospitable reception."

"That answers one question," said Ferguson.

"Now why don't you go away and let Mr. Benson take care of his work?"

"What work?" asked Simmons. "He ain't doin' anything."

Ferguson said coldly: "Mr. Simmons, if you would follow Mr. Benson around for a couple of days and do some real work instead of trying to figure out a way to beat somebody else out of something, you would not ask such a fool question."

Simmons stepped forward. "I take it that's a challenge."

"You're of age," said Ferguson. "Take it any way you like."

Yeakel laid a hand on Simmons' arm. Simmons shrugged it off angrily, but he stayed back.

"Mr. Benson, you'd better go to your mules," said Ferguson. "I hear Teddy Root's foghorn voice across the river."

Benson looked at Ferguson, then at the men facing them, and it was quite obvious that, frightened or upset as he was, he wanted to be there for the showdown — but Ferguson waved him on. "I may have other fish to fry with these gentlemen," said Ferguson, "but the ferry must continue to operate. Otherwise, the eager lambs on yonder shore will not be able to reach Nebraska for the shearing."

Charlie Logan demanded: "What do you mean by that?"

Ferguson watched Benson start up the slope, and he noted that, from somewhere or from nowhere, a crowd had started to gather, for half a dozen men now stood above them on the slope, waiting. A small boy back at the two wagons shouted: "Come on, everybody! There's gonna be a fight!"

Children piled out of the wagons and came running from the brush along the river like drops of water squeezed out of a sponge. Mothers started calling, but Ferguson did not think they would have much luck.

He turned back to the business at hand, noting that Ackerman and Ernest were standing beside him. Ernest could not be much good in a fight, but he seemed willing to try. Ferguson said, "You ever hear of Logan City?"

Nobody answered for a moment, but finally Charlie Logan said, "What about it?"

"Somebody in the East," said Ferguson, "is circulating colored lithographs of Logan City — a town that never existed."

"That's not saying it won't exist," said Yeakel.

"Nor is it saying that it will exist."

"There's no law against drawing up plans," said Logan.

"Maybe there's no law against selling lots in a townsite that doesn't exist," said Ferguson, "but that doesn't make it right."

One of the men from the crowd on the slope walked out toward Ferguson. He wore a big, droopy-brimmed hat, a full black beard, high boots, and a red cowhide vest with the hair on.

"Did I hear you mention Logan City?" he demanded.

Ferguson restrained his satisfaction, for he knew what was going to happen. "You heard of it?" he asked.

"You're damn tootin' right I heard of it." He took a worn, tightly-folded paper from inside his shirt, and began to unfold it — a colored lithograph. "It says down here, 'Logan City, Nebraska Territory.'" He looked up. "Which one of you gents is responsible for that?"

Logan moistened his lips. Yeakel watched, hard-eyed. Simmons swallowed. Wiggins looked across the river.

"Well," said the man, "I asked a question."

Major Yeakel broke the silence. "We don't even know you."

"You don't have to — but my name is Art Grimes, and I come out here from Pennsylvania. I want to know where Logan City is."

"Maybe," said Ackerman, "Charlie Logan would know something about that."

"If he don't," said Ernest, "Major Yeakel will."

"I don't give a damn who it is," said Grimes, "so I find out where the town is."

"There's no town of that name," said Ferguson. "You might as well get used to the idea."

Grimes stared at him. "You mean to say —" He held up the map. "Right here it shows 'Blacksmith Shop,' 'Post Office,' 'Saddlery,'

'Sanitarium,' 'Baptist Church'." He looked up. "It shows all these here places, and I want to know where they are."

"They don't exist," said Ferguson.

"Now that don't make sense," said Grimes. "It shows 'em on this here map, doesn't it?"

"My good man," said Major Yeakel, "anybody can draw a map, and they can print anything on it they want to — but that doesn't prove it exists."

"It better," said Grimes, "for I paid three hundred dollars for a lot on the strength of this map."

"Three hundred!" said a new voice from up on the slope. A man came running to join them, and Ferguson recognized Simon Hudson. "They absolutely swore four hundred dollars was the bottom price — and I bought two."

"What I want to know," said Ackerman, "is who made up this map."

Yeakel said, "A draftsman, of course."

"Who paid for it?"

Yeakel was in no hurry to answer.

"You — Logan!" said Grimes. "It was named after you. Who was in on it?"

"I never intended —"

"Who pocketed my three hundred dollars?"

"I don't know," said Logan.

"Where is the townsite?"

"As far as we know," said Ferguson, "there is no such townsite — and there is no such railroad as the Eastern Nebraska, Omaha & Kansas City."

"No railroad!"

Grimes took four steps toward Logan and Yeakel, and Yeakel said, "My good man, I am armed. Don't start anything."

"If it's necessary," said Grimes coldly, "I'll go back to my wagon and get my rifle."

"Simon!" called the fat woman from the top of the slope. "You come back here!"

Hudson looked, but he did not answer. With somebody to speak up for him, he seemed to have gathered courage.

Yeakel said, "There is no need to get your wind up. This townsite will be laid out just as it is shown here. We are awaiting only a charter from the Nebraska territorial legislature — which is in the process of being granted right now."

"Then what about the churches, and the blacksmith shop, and the sanitarium — and the railroad?"

"All those things will come in time," said Yeakel. "Rome wasn't built in a day."

"Where is this townsite gonna be?" Grimes demanded.

"The exact location is a secret," said Yeakel, "but it will be in this area. And now, my good man, I advise you to go on about your business so we can get to work."

Grimes looked at him levelly. "Mister, *this* is my business. I quit a job; I sold out everything;

and I brung my family all the way out here to settle on this here lot — No. 66."

"Perhaps," said Yeakel, "if you would find something to keep busy at, and give us a chance to develop our plans —"

"I'm givin' you a chance," said Grimes, "but I ain't goin' far, and I want to see some action in thirty days, or else!"

It would have ended peacefully but for Mrs. Hudson. That high, clarion call came again from the top of the slope, and it must have inspired the little man to show off, for suddenly he stepped toward Yeakel and said, "I want my money back. I want my eight hundred dollars and I want it right now."

Charlie Logan lost his patience. "Why don't you go on back and tend to you knittin'?"

The little man bristled. "Mr. Logan," he said, "I paid eight hundred dollars for two lots to start a bakery, and you either show me the lots or give me my money back."

Simmons took a hand — perhaps, thought Ferguson, because he thought he could bluff Hudson. He stepped out to meet him and said, "Come now, let's not create a scene."

"Scene!" Hudson fairly shook with anger. "I paid eight hundred dollars. I got a right to a lot of scenes!"

Yeakel tried to placate him. "My good man, within thirty days, I promise you, we will have definite information for you."

"In thirty days," he told Yeakel, "you could

be in Timbuktu."

"I have no intention whatever of leaving the country. I have a farm here," said Yeakel.

"That don't mean you won't leave," said Grimes.

Hudson stepped forward and shook the lithograph under Yeakel's nose. "This is a townsite. It says it's a townsite. And I paid eight hundred dollars for lots 38 and 40, and I want my lots or my money back — right now!"

It was one of those things hard to figure out. Ferguson doubted that Simon Hudson had ever fought before in his life, but something had gotten into him now — perhaps he had taken a notion to show off in front of his wife; perhaps it was desperation; perhaps it was the country and the air of a man's standing up for his rights. At any rate, he held the lithograph in one hand, and shook his other hand in Yeakel's face. "You heard me! I want some results!"

Simmons took hold of Hudson's arm to turn him away. Hudson whirled, and to Ferguson's amazement he hit Simmons in the left eye with his fist. Simmons hit back; then Yeakel grabbed Hudson's arms from behind, and Simmons, his face hard, let loose a long haymaker that literally lifted the little man off his feet.

It was too much for Ferguson. He seized Simmons by the shoulder and spun him around, met him with a hard, bony fist on the point of the jaw.

Major Yeakel pulled his six-shooter from his waistband, and at that moment Dave Ackerman's big hand swung down and closed over it. Yeakel pulled the trigger, but the shot went into the ground. Then Ackerman had the revolver and hurled it into the river. Yeakel stepped back to defend himself, and Logan rushed in to help him.

Ferguson straightened Simmons with two long, looping rights. Simmons stumbled, but fell back against Ackerman and regained his balance. Ferguson followed him, but Simmons lowered his head and roared in to butt him in the stomach. For a moment Ferguson felt as if there was a vacuum inside him, and all the force in the world was trying to pull his body into the hole. While he bent over, helpless, Simmons poured in everything he had, and Ferguson staggered, limp.

Grimes had gotten into the fight and had picked off Charlie Logan, and closed with him in a bear-wrestle. Logan was wiry, but he was no good at that kind of fighting, and he struggled to get his arms free.

Ackerman was down but trying to get to his knees. Simon Hudson was fighting toe-to-toe with Yeakel.

Logan kicked Grimes in the shins and broke loose; he floundered and came to his balance in front of Ackerman; he kicked Ackerman under the chin which sent him down, then turned to get Hudson away from Yeakel.

Ferguson, straightening in spite of the blows from Simmons, got his arms up high enough to protect his face, and stumbled back to get his breath. He plunged into Simmons and knocked him against Grimes. Ferguson followed Simmons, caught his arm and threw him like a rock from a slingshot. He heard a bone crack as he did so, but then he was into Logan, taking care to keep out of range of Logan's feet. He went in close and literally walked the man over backward, hitting him again and again as fast as he could pump his arms.

Yeakel looked around him and suddenly held up his hands. "All right, I quit," he said.

Simon Hudson backed off, bloody but triumphant. "How about my eight hundred dollars?"

"I don't have eight hundred dollars," said Yeakel. "I will pay you as soon as I can get it."

Ferguson had his own idea when that would be.

The fight was over as abruptly as it had started. Ferguson drew a deep breath and walked down to the dock; the ferry was in the middle of the river, and held a covered wagon and a small herd of cows.

Osterman came riding down the slope. "Looks like you had a big fly-up with Yeakel's outfit," he said.

Ferguson nodded. "That little man, Hudson, is quite a scrapper."

"What over?"

"Hudson wanted his money back." Ferguson

washed his face with river water. "What I don't understand," he said, "is whether they have any land at all for a townsite."

"They got maps," said Osterman.

"Why didn't they call in Patagonia or something?" asked Grimes. "Why did Logan put his name on it?"

"It don't seem sensible," said Osterman.

"The only land they've got, as far as I know, is a quarter for Logan and a quarter for Yeakel. Simmons has none at all, except what he took while Mr. Benson was down here — and he won't have that long. Two quarters are not enough for a townsite, which is generally one or two sections. Nor would they dare to sell lots of their pre-emption land, because the very essence of pre-emption claims is that they are for personal use. A man has to swear to that before he can get a title. So why would he put his name on the lithograph?"

"Maybe he's vain," said Osterman. "Say, you better go to the doctor. You got a bad cut under your eye."

"I always wondered why that Simmons wears a heavy ring," said Ferguson. "Now I know why." He tried to stanch the blood, but it continued to flow. "I'll ride up to the Forks," he decided, "as soon as this ferryload comes in."

While he was waiting, on the extra sheet of brown paper given him by Mr. Weinstein, he wrote out notice of the claim club meeting

83

and laid it on the corner of the dock with a stone on top. That one, and the one in Weinstein's store, ought to be notice enough.

CHAPTER VI

FERGUSON RODE OFF for Turner's Tavern on the way to the Forks.

Sally was in back, tying up marsh grass in tight bundles for winter fuel, and Ferguson dismounted and said, "Afternoon, Miss Sally."

"Good — oh!"

"What's wrong?"

"That terrible cut under your eye."

He shrugged. "It doesn't amount to much."

"Another fight?"

"I guess they're trying to see if they can wear me down."

She came close to him to look at it. "We'd better take care of it."

"I'm willing — but what's to eat?"

"Nothin' just yet," she said.

"Nothin' sure smells good."

She smiled. "A hunter from Omaha City come by with a quarter of buffalo-meat, and pa bought it off him."

"When will it be ready to eat?"

"I put it in the oven right after you left this morning. It ought to be ready for supper."

"Anything for right now?" he asked, reluctant to leave.

"Coffee." She brightened. "How about a can of sardines and crackers?"

"Sounds great. I'll tie my horse in front."

She had already set up the coffee when Ferguson got inside. Tom Turner was sitting in his accustomed corner and said, "I heard you bearded the lions this morning."

"I went down to Chippewa to get a notice in the paper, but Logan wanted me to pay for it."

"Ain't necessary," said Turner. "I posted a notice on the beer-barrel." He motioned.

"I won't worry about it," said Ferguson. "If they want a claim club, they'll be here."

"That feller Hudson was real wrought up," said Turner.

"I guess he was. He tried to whip Major Yeakel a little while ago."

"Him?" Turner's eyes were wide.

"Free-for-all. Nobody hurt."

"I hope you didn't break any more arms. They'd have you up for mayhem. Bad cut you got," added Turner.

"I'm going up to the Forks to get it sewed together. Feels all right."

"I'll put a dressing on it," said Sally.

She brought a pan of warm water and some soft rags, and sponged the dried blood from the cut; her fingers were so gentle he could hardly feel them.

"Has anybody looked in on Noah?" he asked.

"Obie went up before noon. He pulled him up, and they took out the dirt and let down some more planks. Noah said he was past two hundred."

He watched her fold a small bandage, and

asked: "How are you going to stick it on?"

"An emigrant traded a piece of court plaster for a pie," she said, "and you get to have it used on you first."

When Sally had finished, she stood back and said, "You look like an Indian on the warpath."

"I don't feel like it," he said, "though I think those sardines will put some life into me."

"I just made some bread too," she said shyly, "if you would like —"

He smiled broadly. "I knew it wasn't all buffalo I smelled. You can't beat fresh lightbread."

Turner agreed. "Her mother made the best bread I ever et — and Sally's is next."

"I've got lots of time," said Ferguson.

Sally brought the sardines and crackers. "I'll start taking the bread out of the oven now," she said, "but I'll have to butter the crust first. Do you like it hot, Mr. Ferguson?"

"Nothing," he said, "is better than hot lightbread — not even bear meat. Miss Sally, I would wait a week."

"It won't be that long," she said, and presently a great cloud of warm aroma came from the lean-to. By the time he had finished the sardines, she was in the dining-room with two huge slices of bread. "I thought maybe you would like a heel, Mr. Ferguson, so I —"

"Miss Sally," he exclaimed, "how did you know? The heel is always the best part."

He ate the bread, and he knew that Sally was

indeed as good a cook of light-bread as any woman he had ever known. "If you'll let me know the next time you bake, I'll come back for a heel," he said.

She was pleased. "I'll sure do that, Mr. Ferguson." She followed him to the door. "I hope nobody gits scared of you with that big bandage, Mr. Ferguson."

He said, "If they do, I'll tell them you put it on."

The Forks was four miles north of Turner's, and he arrived there in mid-afternoon. The Forks, although without a post office, was bigger than Chippewa City — a small cluster of cabins, one frame house, and two or three false-front business places.

Ferguson tied his horse in front of the apothecary's shop. He passed the window with its strange glass containers of colored water, and went up the stairway on the outside. At the top, a door at his right said: *R. E. Doddridge, M.D.*

He pushed open the door, and Doddridge looked over his glasses at him.

"Howdy, doc."

"Howdy, Mr. Ferguson. It looks as if you might have been in a knife-fight."

"Perhaps it should have been," said Ferguson.

The doctor stood up to examine it. "Somebody put a nice bandage on."

"Sally Turner."

"Real nice girl," smiled Doddridge.

Ferguson winced as Doddridge pulled off the court plaster. "Stuff sure sticks," said Doddridge, looking at the cut. "Hm. Not too deep, but a nasty one. Need a few stitches, I guess."

"Does it really need it, doc?"

"Scared?" Doddridge smiled.

"Well, no —"

"It will heal faster, and there will be less danger of gangrene."

"All right."

"We'll just save this bandage." He laid it on his rolltop desk. "Anybody hurt on the other side?"

"Nothing much past a few bruises, far as I know."

Doddridge took off his business coat and rolled up his sleeves. He was a jovial man with a heavy brown mustache, and he went to a glass case and looked over his glasses at his instruments. He selected some, and finally came back with some curved needles with short silk threads. "Lean back here," he said, "so I can get at you."

Ferguson said, "Haven't you got a pain-killer?"

"Come to think of it — yes, I have." He opened the bottom drawer of his desk. "Seeing as how you own the only ferry in this part of the country, I could give you a little something special." He held up the bottle. "French brandy — had it shipped out here for my own use."

"Looks good to me."

Doddridge got a tin cup out of the instrument case. "Real silky. It's cognac, actually. Has quite a wallop." He poured half a cupful.

Ferguson said, "Doc, I'm sorry to use your private drinkin' liquor to deaden pain."

Doddridge chuckled. "What do you think I use it for?"

"Put the cork back in and hide it," said Ferguson. "I won't need any more."

Doddridge put it in the instrument case instead. "I'll need a little when I get through with you." He watched Ferguson down the brandy. "Feel it yet?" he asked presently.

"My upper lip is getting numb already. You can go ahead."

"I'll give you another two or three minutes. Hear you've had lots of trouble at the ferry."

"Quite a bit."

"Any particular reason?"

"Hard to say."

"And if you could, you wouldn't?"

"It's a thing that has to be worked out," said Ferguson. "I'll handle it the best I can."

"I hear you specialize in breaking bones."

"It happened twice," said Ferguson, "but not by my intention. They shouldn't fight with me if they don't want to fight rough."

"I'm sure they will do it to you if you don't do it to them."

"No question about it." He lay back and closed his eyes. "I'm ready."

He felt the doctor cushion his head; the back of his head against Doddridge's stomach. "This will hurt," said Doddridge. "It takes some force to put that needle through your flesh, so hold your head as steady as you can."

Ferguson did not answer. He felt the first needle go through, and felt Doddridge tying the thread; the pull of the thread against his flesh hurt more than the needle, but he hung on to the arms of the chair. He heard the door open, several persons come in, and the door close. Doddridge took the second stitch and began to tie it up. "You gents wait around a few minutes," Doddridge said absently, "and I'll take care of you."

Ferguson did not open his eyes. He heard the newcomers spread around him, and Doddridge took the third stitch. Then he went back to the instrument case, and Doddridge's voice sounded in Ferguson's ears: "You gents here again? It looks like you got troubles again."

Ferguson opened his eyes. Logan was at his right, Yeakel was at his left. He turned; Simmons was behind him, one arm hanging loose. "You follow me up here?" Ferguson asked.

"We came for professional services," said Yeakel.

"I know now why Simmons wears that big

ring on his right hand — and I will remember it the next time we meet."

"No hard feelings," said Simmons.

Ferguson said dryly, "It is not a question of hard feelings. It is a question of accepting or not accepting your dictation."

"These are the growing pains of a community," Logan began, "and —"

He looked at Logan. "Tell me one thing: how can you ever get a townsite from the legislature? Your land is pre-emption land and you can never sell it off as lots."

Logan said, "We are told that the legislature will grant the charter, and I don't argue with facts."

Yeakel said, "Mr. Ferguson, I will make you an offer for the ferry. We both know that the ferry is the key to this part of Nebraska. There are only five ferries across the Missouri where it bounds Nebraska territory, and this is the only one north of Omaha City. There is a panic in the East, and everybody is moving west. The ferry will make money; we both know that. And if there is a townsite, the ferry will be entry-point for settlers and for all the supplies that will be needed."

"I knew all that some time ago."

"So did I," said Yeakel. "I am merely recapitulating so all the cards will be on the table. I will make you a good offer, Ferguson. I will buy your land which you do not own, and I will buy the ferry and your license, and I will give you four thousand dollars in cash."

Ferguson said, "You told Hudson you didn't have eight hundred dollars in cash."

Yeakel said shortly, "What else can you tell a fanatic?"

"You could tell him the truth."

"I did. If he is patient, he will get his lots."

"When your agent took his money, did he say anything about patience?"

"Mr. Ferguson," said Yeakel, "lots are being sold by the thousands in Nebraska territory and in Kansas, in exactly this fashion."

"That doesn't make it right," Ferguson said stubbornly.

"Still there is no point in singling me out to wage a reform campaign."

Doddridge came back. "You gentlemen look healthy enough."

"We're fine, except that Mr. Simmons has a broken arm."

Doddridge looked at it. "How bad is it?"

"It hurts," said Simmons.

"I had one like this yesterday."

"You'll have more if you keep Ferguson going," said Logan.

Ferguson sat up straight. "If others come looking for trouble, instead of wanting to use the ferry peaceably —"

"Trouble or no," said Yeakel, "you're a bone-breaking expert."

Ferguson sat back.

"What's your answer, Ferguson? Four thousand dollars cash."

Doddridge was trying to thread one of the curved needles.

Ferguson said, "The answer is no."

"On the other hand," Yeakel said casually, "if you do not sell at a fair price, then of course I will be compelled to force you out of business."

"You're trying that now."

"You underestimate me, Mr. Ferguson. When I try to run you away from the ferry, it will be over in a hurry."

"If you are successful."

"I will be successful, Mr. Ferguson — and it will not be too difficult. Think for a moment of Zachariah Mawson and his 12,000 sheep."

"What about them?"

"That is a great many sheep," said Yeakel. "and my guess is that they can be manipulated to tie up the ferry indefinitely, while people on the other side are forced to move on to find another crossing."

"This is a new country," said Ferguson, "and people come out here for a new start, and I think they are entitled to at least equal odds. So I am not selling the ferry to you at any price. And whether these people go somewhere else or not while I move sheep, it is not going to cost me too much. There will always be more people coming."

"Even so, you'd better think about it," said Yeakel.

Doddridge pulled Ferguson's head back against his stomach. The needle went in, and the door opened again while Doddridge was tying the thread.

"Mr. Newcomb, the Indian agent," said Yeakel. "A pleasure to see you here."

"I saw you come up here," said Newcomb, "and I thought I could speak to you about the Otos."

"Oh, yes, the Otos."

"They've been kicked around a lot, and they're going to be hard to hold. They know they have been awarded land on this side of the river, and they're impatient, but I expect the removal to be orderly."

Simmons said, "Injuns are Injuns. If they start running loose over here, there will be scalpin' and massacrin'."

"Not with the Otos," said Ferguson.

"An Injun is a redskin," said Simmons. "They are all alike, and I would not trust one of the dirty, stinkin', filthy —"

The Indian agent said patiently, "The Otos are warriors by heritage; their chief was Black Bird, and they have a long and proud history, and should not be looked down on as shiftless Indians. If they are left alone, they will harm nobody, but if they are mistreated, they will fight back."

"They're still Injuns," muttered Simmons.

"Walking Bird is a grandson of Black Bird, and he knows the handwriting on the wall. He is controlling his people, but even Walking Bird has a limit to his patience."

"What do you want us to do?" asked Logan.

"Merely leave them alone. Walking Bird won't let them steal or molest any white man or his property, and there will be no trouble unless some hot-head or some person starts it without thinking."

"With Injuns," Simmons insisted, "you don't have to start nothin'."

Newcomb spoke to Yeakel and Logan. "If you gentlemen have any influence over your friend here, I hope you will help him see the light. If the Indians should go on the warpath, a lot of whites will be killed. The Indians, of course, will be wiped out, but a lot of whites will be killed before it is over."

"We'll do what we can," said Yeakel, who obviously was not very much concerned.

"I stopped a man named Keller. Any of you know him?"

"What did he do?" asked Logan.

"He was drinking — saw one of Walking Bird's men and started after him with a knife."

"How'd you stop him?" asked Yeakel.

"Tripped him," said Newcomb, "then got the Indian out of sight." He shook his head. "With men like that on the loose, it's almost an impossible situation."

But Ferguson did not feel hopeful about men like Yeakel and Logan; they were in a position to help avoid trouble, but he knew that neither of them wanted to.

CHAPTER VII

FERGUSON WAS BACK at his place by supper time. He went to the well, ascertained that Noah was all right, and caught the mule to bring him up.

"It got a mite damp down there this afternoon," said Noah. "We might have water."

"It's pretty early," said Ferguson. "Most of them go to around three hundred. Anyway, we can tell in the morning. Maybe we'll find fifty feet of water in the hole, and you'll be through digging."

"I'd just as soon," said Noah.

"Anybody come by?"

Noah was brushing the dirt from his clothes. "Yes, sir, Obie pulled me up for a breath of fresh air, and a fellar came by lookin' for you."

"Know his name?"

"Never seen him before. Had on buckskin shirt with long fringes — didn't look like he'd ever been in an Injun fight."

"Why?"

"None of the thrums was cut off for waddin'."

"I think I know who you mean: A real handsome fellow, rode a dun horse?"

Noah tipped up the water jug. "That's him."

"What did he have to say?"

"Nothin' much, I guess. He just come from

the tavern, and he was talkin' about Sally."

Ferguson looked up sharply.

"He wanted to know who owned this place, and he said they were going to take 160 acres away from everybody who had 320."

"Who is going to do that?"

Noah put the jug down and piped his mouth on the back of his arm. "He didn't say, I guess. Something about the territorial legislature."

"Which allows 320 acres."

Noah looked up at him thoughtfully. "Maybe — but he said the gover'ment only allows 160."

"Somebody has been telling him about the law."

Noah pointed. "It looks like you're gonna have company, Mr. Ferguson."

A single rider on a bay horse was coming across the prairie from the general direction of Mrs. Talbot's place. "So it seems," said Ferguson.

"Is it true, then? Pa claims 320. Does that mean he will lose it?"

"I don't think so."

"But if the gover'ment —"

"The government has not done anything yet and it has usually turned out that those who settle on a reasonable amount of land get to keep it — if they can hold it until the government gets there."

"Is that why you're goin' to have a claim club?"

"That's about it. Now, you'd better head for

home. Sally has buffalo roast on for supper."

"So long, Mr. Ferguson."

"So long." Ferguson could not yet identify the rider approaching, but he thought it looked like a woman, for she seemed to be riding side-saddle. He knew of no woman in the country who might be riding except Mrs. Talbot, and he wondered why she would want to see him.

Mrs. Talbot rode up on the bay, and he walked to meet her.

"I'm sorry for my rude treatment of you today," she said, "and I came to apologize."

He smiled. "No apology necessary."

"I brought a peace offering." She handed him a tin bucket covered with a clean dishtowel. It felt warm to his hands.

"Smells good," he said. "What is it?"

"Roast buffalo," she said. "I bought some from a hunter." She smiled. "I know how a man is, living by himself. He doesn't like to cook and he doesn't eat right. I made some light-bread too."

"Smells good," he said again.

He bit through the crunchy crust, and found it much like Sally's; in fact, he could not have told them apart.

She said, "If you'd like some coffee, I'll make some for you."

She went into his house, and soon he heard her voice from the back door. "Coffee's ready."

He sat down and she set a place for him.

She laid out the food, and it looked good —

three thick slices of light-bread and a huge chunk of roast meat. He pulled the box to the table. "I'm sorry I haven't better chairs. Aren't you having coffee, too?"

She got another cup.

"How did you ever get into Nebraska in the first place?" he asked.

"I didn't intend to come here. It was one of those things that I couldn't help. My little sister and I were orphaned when our father and mother went through the ice on the Hudson in a cutter."

"Your parents had money, then."

"Enough to be comfortable, but it all disappeared by the time I was of age. My aunt's husband handled it, and I think he wanted us girls just so he could get his hands on the property."

He chewed a juicy mouthful of buffalo meat. "What happened then?"

"Jerome — Mr. Talbot — had been courting us both. I think —" She sipped the coffee. "I think he wanted to get his own hands on the money." She paused briefly.

"I reached my twenty-first birthday, and he proposed. I didn't really want to get married, and I put him off, but then I found out that my parents' money was gone, and I married him without saying anything about it." She stared at the table. "He was furious when I told him."

"But you liked him anyway?"

"What else could I do? I was married, I was

of age, and I had no tie anywhere except to my sister."

He tried the coffee, and found it good.

"It turned out that he couldn't even make a living for us. We went to St. Louis, and he tried various things — but he wasn't even a good dock-hand."

"Then you heard about the free land in Nebraska."

"We came out here, as you know, and took a pre-emption claim a few days after you did. Then Jerome went down to Council Bluffs City for supplies, with what little money we had left, and came back without a cent, thinking he could bluff you into letting him cross for nothing."

Ferguson looked up. "I would have, if he had come clean with me — but he tried to argue the right and wrong of it."

"I know. He was always that way."

"He was a nasty fighter, too. I couldn't get rid of him without doing — what I did."

"It was a terrible way to die — but he had earned it."

"Your sister," he said. "You encouraged her to follow you?"

She looked at the candle. "She was alone, and they were not good to her after I found out about the money, so she got married to Henry Wiggins." She looked bleakly at Ferguson. "He is not a fourflusher like Jerome, but he is a little man and very vain. It is his ambition to have people look up to him — but he is a blunderer. Nobody will ever look up to him — not even Ethel."

"Why did he provoke a fight with me this morning?"

She shook her head. "I don't know. I know that Yeakel and Simmons took him to the Forks to get his arm fixed. I have an idea that they talked to him on the other side of the river and offered him some money to whip you."

He looked hard at her, then he moved around the table and took her in his arms; she was surprisingly solid and yet yielding. He held her hard against him, and presently she looked up at him in that stark, challenging way and he kissed her. He picked her up, still kissing him, and carried her to the bed. But as he started to put her down, she said, "No."

He thought it nothing but a womanly protest, and held her for a moment, his hand on her bare thigh beneath her dress. She clung to him, but as he moved to undress her she cried frantically, "No!"

"Why not?" he wanted to know.

"It isn't me you want. You are grateful for the food and for my company, but it isn't me you want."

"I want you or I would not have brought you to the bed."

She said, "I want you. Oh, I can't tell you how much I want you — but we will have to wait."

"Wait for what?"

"Wait until you are sure you want me." She looked starkly at him again. "When you are sure, you may have me."

"Would you like me to ride home with you?"

She said in a low voice: "And go through this again? Once is enough in one night, Mr. Ferguson."

"I am rather concerned over your going home alone. There are so many new and unknown persons in the country . . ."

"Please do not think of it. Really —" She put her hand on his for an instant. "I don't need help to find my way home. And I am not scared."

He stood there for a while and listened to the bay's hooves fade rapidly in the soft dirt. Then he went into the cabin, blew out the candle, and lay down on the grass mattress. He did not go to sleep for a long time, and when he did, it seemed that he had hardly closed his eyes when he heard somebody pounding on the door, and Mr. Benson's excited voice:

"Mr. Ferguson! Wake up! Something's happened to the ferry!"

CHAPTER VIII

HE GOT UP groggily. Mr. Benson was inside by that time, and Ferguson looked for a light in the stove, found it had burned out, and got a block of sulphur matches from the box on the wall. "Now what happened to the ferry?" he asked.

"I went down at three o'clock to open it as usual, and I found the rope broke and the ferry drifted over to the other side. I couldn't get Teddy Root up, and anyway, I guess it calls for you to make the decisions, Mr. Ferguson." He looked at the bandage on Ferguson's face and said, "Was it from that last fight?"

Ferguson hesitated, remembering that Mrs. Talbot had not commented on the bandage. Finally he said, "I had it sewed up. When did the ferry get loose?" He began to pull on his trousers in the dark.

"I closed down the ferry at eleven-thirty last night, and it's three-thirty now," said Benson.

"How did you get here?"

"On the mule — and I think I better take the other one back and let this one rest for a few days. Seems like it takes about two teams to keep the ferry going."

"It's hard work — too hard, maybe. You were at it yesterday for twenty hours." He said thoughtfully, "No Horse could run the ferry if they would let him."

"They wouldn't stand for it," said Benson. "A man like Keller —"

"Too bad. But no matter — you have got to get some rest."

"I gener'ly get my nap in the afternoon when you're there. I ain't hurt, Mr. Ferguson. I don't feel as old as I look, maybe."

He was almost pathetic in his eagerness to stay on the job, and Ferguson said, "All right — but don't keep working until you drop. Those people can wait till tomorrow."

His voice quavered. "You paid me for doin' a job, Mr. Ferguson, and I aim to do it as long as I can."

"You don't need to kill yourself."

Benson said earnestly, "Mr. Ferguson, I never amounted to nothin' back home; I couldn't even keep up my taxes. I come out here to start over, and I'm aimin' to stay with it."

Ferguson pulled on his boots. "All right, Mr. Benson, but don't try to do any fighting."

"I ain't scared."

"I am, Mr. Benson. I want to see you live to raise a corn crop."

"You don't think they'd kill anybody?"

Ferguson said, "Did you take time to put the coffeepot on the fire down at the ferry?"

"I built up the fire and put some more river water in the grounds."

Ferguson went outside under the stars. He

wondered briefly it Mrs. Talbot was awake.

"Do you want I should turn the mule loose?" asked Benson.

"Take off the bridle. I will get the sorrel out to go behind the other mule. You will have to ride double with me back to the ferry, because this mule won't take anything on her back."

He caught up the mule without any trouble, and led her back to the house. Benson threw a saddle on her, and bridled her.

Benson had filled the barrel-butt with water, and Ferguson listened to the worn-out mule drink noisily. "Is there plenty of rope at the ferry?" he asked.

"There's a couple of coils and a lot of short pieces, besides the one that broke."

They started out, the animals' hooves clip-clapping on the hard sod. Benson motioned toward a yellow light in the distance. "Tom Turner's girl gets up early too. They serve meals to the emigrants in the morning."

"It's a hard-working family," said Ferguson thoughtfully.

They saw the red-glowing fire of buffalo-chips (because all wood in the vicinity had long been used up), and presently they were close enough to see the blue flame above it. Benson dismounted and unsaddled the mule and staked her; he broke one of the chips, two feet in diameter, and put it on the fire. Ferguson unsaddled the sorrel and staked it; he went under one end of an Osnaburg canvas and got an armful of hay, and split it between the two animals. Then he went to the fire and accepted the cup that Benson offered him. He tried it, found it too hot, and stood for a moment, staring into the darkness across the river. "Fires starting up over there," he said. "Emigrants will be coming down to the ferry."

"It won't hurt 'em to wait a couple of hours," said Benson.

"They don't want to wait, Mr. Benson. They want to get to the promised land."

Benson sat back on his heels. "They won't reach it when they figgered."

"And I guess it won't hurt them," said Ferguson absentmindedly. "Why do you suppose that rope broke during the night, with no load on the ferry?"

"Worn, maybe."

"Not worn enough to break." He finished the coffee and walked up to the dock and onto it, his boots thudding on the boards and producing hollow sounds from the cavernous space beneath the dock. He made out the rope in the faint light from the fire, reached down and picked it up. "It didn't break," he said. "It was cut."

Benson hurried out on the dock. "You sure, Mr. Ferguson?"

"A broken rope is frayed at the end. This one is not frayed," he said. "Feel it. It is cut off square, as if somebody had used an axe."

"The dirty so-and-so's," said Benson. "Why

would they do a thing like that?"

Ferguson said, "This is only the beginning, Mr. Benson."

"Maybe you'd be better off to string with Logan and Yeakel."

Ferguson grinned wryly in the dark. "When I'm in the right, I've never had enough gumption to run."

He chose a coil of half-inch rope, measured it and counted the coils, and decided it was long enough to reach across the river. He saddled the sorrel and tied the end of the rope to the saddlehorn. He stationed Benson on the dock to see that it would uncoil properly, and he took the precaution of tying the other end to a post on the dock. He got on the sorrel and rode into the water; the sorrel was a good river-horse, and the river in late June was low, so that it would not be necessary to swim except in the middle of the stream. They reached the ferry, swinging at the end of the rope from the Iowa side, and he got aboard and examined it as well as he could, for down on the river it was still almost dark. He called to Benson and presently, finding nothing further wrong with the ferry, he got on again, his wet trousers not sliding very well on the leather, and rode on through the reeds and willows to the shore. He kept going in a straight line, for now the rope was running across the deck of the ferry. He went up the bank and found himself among half a dozen small fires, each by a covered wagon; he reflected that at least they had learned to save wood.

But he had just felt a harder pull that meant that the big ferry towrope was coming across the river, when a man looked up from a fire where he was holding a strip of beef on a pointed stick, saw Ferguson, and came to meet him, walking clumsily in cowhide boots.

"Are you from the ferry, mister?"

"Yes."

"I'm Reverend Sledge from West Virginia," he said in a twangy voice. "Here with a wife, six young'uns, two cows, four mules, and a saddle horse."

"All right." Ferguson started on.

"Wait, mister." The big man laid a hand on the saddle. "I got a question to ask you."

Ferguson waited.

"We been here four days, and we're next out for the ferry."

"You'd better start packing."

"But the ferry broke loose and has been against the bank all night."

It was then that Ferguson heard sheep. He said to the man: "It will be in service in a couple of hours at the most." The sorrel moved impatiently.

"I don't like to be insistent, mister, but I want my turn."

"That's not my responsibility," said Ferguson. "We leave that for the emigrants to settle among themselves — and as far as I have heard, they are generally fair."

Teddy Root loped up on a mangy mustang that he had traded from the Otos. "Mr. Ferguson, anything serious?"

"Not as far as I have seen."

"Some of the emigrants are fussing."

"Fussing does not help," Ferguson said.

"They are asking why you shut down three or four hours a night."

"To get some rest," said Ferguson.

The Reverend Sledge said: "Mr. Ferguson, you own this ferry, I hear. Why don't you hire two more men, and keep open all night?"

Ferguson sat sidewise in the wet saddle. "There are two reasons, reverend. The first is that there are no men old enough to run the ferry by themselves, and there are not enough mules in the country to pull it. I have every mule I can get in use right now.

"Why not oxen?" asked Reverend Sledge. "I use oxen, and they pull real good."

Ferguson ignored him.

He slapped the sorrel with the loose end of the reins, and the sorrel dug in and moved forward slowly.

"Mr. Root, will you go back to the ferry and give a holler when the big rope comes aboard!"

"Yes, sir."

The rope trailed out behind him, and he thought again that he heard sheep, but then Teddy Root shouted from the ferry. Ferguson went twenty feet farther and then turned and rode back, coiling the half-inch rope on his arm as he went. He reached the barge, and Teddy had untied the two ropes and was trying to tie a bowline on the iron ring at the end of the ferry. Ferguson helped him.

It was fairly light then, and Teddy looked up at him, puzzled. "Mr. Ferguson, what happened to the guideline?"

Ferguson looked at him for a moment. "I had forgotten about that," he said. "Of course they cut that too."

"Cut, did you say?"

"Look at the end of the rope you just tied."

"Yes, sir. Sure enough. Now who would be ornery enough to do a lowdown thing like that?"

Ferguson said, "I can guess, but it would be only a guess. Now, Mr. Root, you go back to the dock and pay out the rope on your side slowly when the boat begins to move out into the middle. Don't try to straighten it up. You can straighten up your rope after the ferry reaches the other side."

The reverend's booming voice reached him: "Why not take a load aboard now, Mr. Ferguson?"

"You can't load in here in the swamp grass, and we could not pull it along the shore because of the sandbars. All right, Mr. Benson," he called. "Take it away."

Within a few minutes, the big rope tightened and the ferry began to end around toward the middle of the river. Ferguson gathered up the rest of the half-inch rope and coiled it all on the ferry. Teddy Root got off the ferry and waded through the water to shore, while Ferguson rode up a piece and then out into the water until he picked up the guiderope. He pulled it up to the end, and found that it too was cut square across. He rode back to the shore and began to coil the rope on the sorrel's rump, when he became aware of the bleating sheep again, and finally turned to Teddy Root and asked sharply, "Mr. Root, what is that?"

"There's a feller here with some sheep, wants acrost on the ferry."

"He will have to wait his turn," said Ferguson.

"I tried to tell him," said Teddy, "but he wouldn't listen."

"I will tell him," said Ferguson, "and he will listen. This is not a sheep-ferry. They can swim their sheep if they want across. There is a band of sheep three days back that I have contracted to take across, and that is all. Emigrants have first claim."

They rode up to the dock together. The sun was almost ready to come up, and down the river rolled a wall of heavy fog that was almost on them when Ferguson heard a new, harsh voice, like a man talking through sandpaper: "Ferguson?"

He turned to a black-hatted man who was a full two inches taller than Ferguson, and had shoulders that seemed as wide as an oxbow. "What do you want?" Ferguson asked.

"I was told I might find you here."

Ferguson watched the big rope, now straight, slowly move upstream, then pivoted on the snubbing-post. "I am tired of riddles," he said. "If you have something to say, say it. If you have something to ask, ask it. Otherwise, I'll be obliged if you will stand aside and let me go ahead with my work."

"They said you was a smart one, Ferguson."

Ferguson said, "Mr. Root, I think you might loosen the rope now. Take a half-hitch around the post, and you can let it out as you see fit."

The bleating of the sheep was louder as the fog rolled over them, somewhere up a hill, Ferguson supposed. "Are those your sheep?" he asked.

"They are," said the big man.

"Then you'd better get them away from these hills before the emigrants start a vigilance committee."

"I am here on business. I want passage for my sheep."

"I am not hauling any more sheep," Ferguson said firmly.

"You *are* hauling mine."

"I have made one contract to take some sheep across the river, and that is the last band I will take."

"You will take mine."

Ferguson faced him through the fog. "Mister,

I don't want to be rude, but you are pushing my patience to its limit. I promised one man named Mawson, and —"

"I am Zachariah Mawson," said the man in his grating voice.

"You are not Mawson, he is two days back."

"I am Mawson, and I am damned sick of all this talk, Ferguson. Are you going to take my sheep across or aren't you?"

"You are not Mawson. He had more sheep."

Mawson smiled. "Don't I have enough?" The fog was already lifting, and the sun broke over the horizon to speed it up. Ferguson said, "How could you move that many sheep so far in one day?"

The big man shrugged and smiled cynically. "How do you know where I was two days ago?"

Ferguson went over to watch the rope. He heard footsteps and looked around to see the Reverend Sledge on the dock, accompanied by four other men, emigrants all, by the look of them — high boots, droopy hats, overalls, and checked shirts.

Sledge said: "Ferguson, we come to demand that you carry us in our regular order."

"I intend to."

Mawson grinned. The fog had lifted and thinned, and the area was suddenly clean and sunny, and now Ferguson saw why the bleating of the sheep had come from so many different directions: all the hills within sight were covered by thousands of woolly backs. Mawson looked at Sledge. "Either I take my sheep across, or they will have to be herded on these hills."

CHAPTER IX

FERGUSON REFRAINED FROM any expression
when he looked at Sledge. "Reverend, it looks
like you get a chance to decide for yourself."

One of the men with Mawson said, "Them
sheep will eat up ev'rything green within miles
— and they will stink like h— Pardon me, reverend."

Sledge drew a deep breath and faced the
huge man. "Mister, you are interfering with the
rights of human beings."

Mawson said, "I'm a human being too, reverend. I've got sheep here, and they can't go
hungry, can they?"

"Nobody told you to bring those sheep in
here without first making arrangements for
passage," he said.

"It's a free country. I got as much right to
bring sheep as you got to take your kids."

Ferguson had to hand it to Sledge: he didn't
back down.

"No, you don't. My children are my family."

Mawson was complacent, because he could
not lose. "Reverend, you better call your flock
together around here and decide whether you
want to move now or be et out. And remember
one thing; a few will get across, but them that
stay behind had better start feedin' grain."

That of course was a telling blow, for the emigrants did not carry any grain for the stock; they depended entirely on grass.

Ferguson looked at Sledge and felt a little sorry for him. Sledge was the next man across; if he should give up his place, he might wait several days, and the fact was that the effect of the sheep's presence would be felt immediately, even if the emigrants should wait. On the other hand, if Sledge should insist on his right to cross, the man behind him would then become first and would also insist, and there would be no end to it — so naturally all those down the line would look to the Reverend Sledge to do the right thing.

Sledge's blue eyes blazed for a moment, but he got control of himself; then the light in his eyes was replaced by the dullness of frustration. He said slowly, "I will have to consult the people who are waiting."

Mawson watched him stalk silently away, and turned to Ferguson with sardonic amusement: "The reverend will find out that most people are more interested in gettin' across the river than they are in savin' their souls."

Ferguson looked at Mawson and said, "You are an overriding and unfair man."

"What do you care?" asked Mawson. "Are they any kin of yours?"

Ferguson said slowly: "Your kind of man would recognize only one thing: somebody who could lick you."

Mawson grinned. "A lot have tried that —

and some of them weighed twice as much as you."

Ferguson said, "I will move your sheep in whatever order the emigrants decide, but I don't like your methods and I won't stand for them to be applied to me."

The black eyes were sardonic again. "How long do you figure it will take to cross my sheep?" asked Mawson.

"How many head?"

"Close to twelve thousand."

"Well, it's a good-sized ferry, and it will carry a hundred and fifty head. At twenty round trips a day, that's three thousand head a day — four days." He looked at Mawson. "You would be better off to swim them across, at that. You could get them across in one day, and you could hire help from the emigrants and save about nine hundred dollars."

"There's too much loss in swimming."

"There needn't be. I can swim those critters across and guarantee less than a quarter per cent loss."

But Mawson wanted the sheep to cross on the ferry. "If a sudden rise came up —"

"There aren't any rises like that, this time of year."

Something flickered in Mawson's eyes. "My man made a deal with you at eight cents a head. I'm holding you to it."

Ferguson said quietly, "Your man also told me you were two days back, and I will not take you before that time unless the emigrants agree to it."

"They will agree," said Mawson. "They're already down on their prayer-bones."

The tone of his voice was more than Ferguson could take. "You've no right to ridicule a man for doing what you order when you hold a pistol at his head."

"Ain't I, though?"

"You ain't," Ferguson said positively.

He saw a new light — a hard and antagonistic glint — in the man's eyes. He turned away to watch Teddy Root letting the rope spiral slowly around the post as the ferry neared the Nebraska shore. "Now, then," said Ferguson, "when Mr. Benson gives you the signal that all is well, you can prepare to pull the ferry back to this dock for the first loading, but meantime I will go back across the river with the guiderope. Otherwise you and No Horse would have to balance the mules against each other to keep the boat from swinging downstream against the bank again — either that or control the rope by the snubbing-post — and that would wear out two good men in their prime."

"Maybe there ain't no good men in Nebrasky," said Mawson.

Ferguson looked at him. "Maybe there are no good men in Iowa," he said.

Ferguson went to the sorrel and picked up the cut end of the guiderope. "See that it's paid out," he said, and pushed the sorrel into the water.

He reached the other side and rode up onto dry land. Benson took the rope and spliced a piece onto it, then fastened it to its ring. Benson was an ex-sailor and knew his knots.

"Drop your towrope," Ferguson said, "and we'll try it again."

Up the slope, No Horse disengaged the rope from the doubletree, dropped the trace chains so the mules could graze on the scanty grass, and started back down. Ferguson called across the river: "All right, Mr. Root."

Benson came up and said, "Sounds like I hear singin'."

"Very likely," said Ferguson.

" 'Rock of Ages', sounds like."

"Probably."

Benson looked up at him. "Sandy John Ferguson, you know what's going on."

"I can guess."

"You might tell me," said Benson, sounding aggrieved.

"The Reverend Sledge is calling on the Lord for guidance — which means that if, by the time prayer meeting is over, he can figure out a way to best Zachariah Mawson, he will do it, but if he cannot figure out a way, he will advise the brethern to turn the other cheek."

The ferry began to move away from the dock, and the rope trailed after it.

"What are they up to?" asked Benson.

"Prayin' for another ferry?"

"I don't know what they're praying for, but I know what they're wishing: that Zachariah Mawson would take his sheep somewhere else and give them away to the Indians."

"I thought I saw sheep over there, and I *sure* smelled 'em."

"Reverend Sledge is wrestling with his patience," said Ferguson, walking to the coffeepot, "but I don't think he can win. He wants across the river because he figures the free land is going fast, but he's really a sincere man, and I think he will have trouble justifying what he would like to do, so I expect a load of sheep."

"Whyn't you go over on the ferry, then?"

Ferguson looked down at his wet clothes. "And take a chance on getting dried out?" He watched across the river for a moment, where the Reverend Sledge's temporary congregation was now on its knees in prayer, and the stentorian voice of the Reverend Sledge rose and fell in measured cadence. "When they make their decision, I'll go over and show them how to get the sheep onto the ferry."

"You're pretty sure," said Benson.

"It's the only way it can go." He looked around. "Where's our audience this morning?"

"Major Yeakel and Simmons came lookin' for you while you was gone. I told them where you was, and they went away."

Ferguson said, half to himself, "I wonder what they were up to?"

"Charlie Logan said they wanted an understanding with you about No Horse."

"What's to be understood?"

"They said No Horse was drinkin' and makin' threats."

"Mr. Benson, have you smelled liquor on his breath?" asked Ferguson.

"Sure not lately," said Benson.

The ferry was nearing the other shore, and the group of kneeling emigrants began to break up. Sledge walked to the dock where Mawson stood, a giant of a man even at such a distance. There was some talk which Ferguson could not make out, and then Mawson shouted and fired his six-shooter twice into the air, and on one of the green hills covered with sheep, men and dogs began to move. The ferry stopped at the dock, and Teddy Root began to tie up. The sheep were moving down toward the meadow, and presently the herders got them squeezed down to something resembling a column. Ferguson caught up the sorrel, threw a saddle on it, and rode into the water

He walked the sorrel out on dry land before the sheep were within a quarter of a mile. Mawson was standing on the dock, grinning superciliously. "Not even the will of the Lord," he said, "can prevail against the smell of twelve thousand sheep."

Ferguson looked at him steadily. "There are other things that stink worse," he said.

The big man took a breath, and his chest

swelled out. "You and me will have a settlement after we get the sheep across," he said. "I will whip you till your own mother won't recognize you."

"I have no mother here, Mr. Mawson," Ferguson said, and turned away to Teddy Root. "Mr. Root, we shall have to set the posts along the sides and ends, and run a rope through them."

Teddy Root nodded. "The posts are down there by the mule shed."

"Take the mule with you — and bring a coil of half-inch rope. We'll have to build a fence so the sheep won't walk off."

"We'll sure have to scrub the ferry when we get through, too, or the horses won't walk on it."

Ferguson sighed. "We may have to burn it."

Mawson went down to meet the sheep, and Root took the mule to get the stakes and the rope. Ferguson examined the guiderope to see that it was in its three iron rings on the upstream side of the ferry, and then walked after Mawson toward the approaching sheep. At the head of the column were four men, and for an instant Ferguson stopped short. The four men were all huge, wore black hats, and were exact duplicates of Zachariah Mawson, only twenty years or so younger.

Ferguson became aware that Mawson was watching him, for now he laughed shortly and said, "Ferguson, these are my four boys. They can't whip me yet, but they can whip anybody else."

"Have you got a head sheep?" asked Ferguson.

"We had an old ewe," said the youngest boy, "but she died."

"What's your name?" asked Ferguson.

"Abner." The boy was about twenty years old.

"You got names for the rest of 'em?" asked Ferguson.

Mawson scowled. "Abner, Dutch, Henry, and Matt. Matt's the oldest and the biggest."

"Well," said Ferguson, "since there's no lead sheep, we'll see if we can find one. Meantime, we'll have to get them on board the best way we can. You fellows cut out a hundred and fifty and we'll see what happens."

The four boys looked at their father, and he nodded. It was obvious that he made the decisions, and that was worth knowing.

Two of the boys stayed alongside the front of the column to act as pointers; the other two went back to cut out the first load. They worked their way into the sheep and began to drive them forward. Teddy Root stood in the middle of the dock at the far side of the entrance to the ferry; the rope was in place.

Ferguson noted half a dozen emigrants watching, and motioned to them. "If you fellows want this to get over with as soon as possible, spread yourselves along the dock and steer the sheep onto the ferry. Don't shout or wave your arms unless you have to; just stand and keep quiet."

Sledge stepped forward. "Mr. Ferguson, we have been euchred out of our birthright, and we have submitted to it in the name of Christianity, but we recognize no obligation to put our shoulders to the wheel of the man who ran us off the road."

"All right," said Ferguson. He hoped they had no intention of interfering.

A sheep trotted forward on the dock, hesitated, went to the edge, saw the water, turned away. Ferguson moved up, squeezing it toward the ferry. Teddy Root backed up a little to give the sheep a chance to go through the roped opening onto the ferry. The sheep ran around in a circle, darted past Root to the end of the dock, then wheeled and returned. Ferguson headed it away from the approaching band, which stopped dead as if it had been a single unit. The sheep tried to go past Ferguson, who got in its way; it ran back toward Root, looked at the entrance-way to the ferry, then suddenly wheeled and dashed straight at Ferguson, who tried to stop it. That time, however, it refused to be side-tracked. It ran straight at him, caught him off-balance, got his legs tangled up, and left him on his face on the dock while it leaped into the water and splashed off downstream.

When two of the Mawson boys ran to catch the runaway, the rest of the sheep surged forward and broke into a dash down the dock. Ferguson got to his feet in a hurry and leaped to one side. Teddy Root stepped onto the ferry, and the sheep lumbered to the edge of the dock. There the foremost animals stopped, but those behind pressed on and pushed the first ones over the edge into the water. A moment later, twenty sheep were in the water; Mawson was cursing, and Sledge was looking on, stony-faced. Ferguson shouted at Mawson, "Send a couple of men!" and the other two boys got Mawson's nod and ran forward into the water.

Ferguson concentrated on those that were left, trying to steer them onto the ferry, but the first ranks would go only to the entrance, then wheel and make for the opposite side of the dock.

Two boys had recovered the first sheep, but the other two were floundering in the water, shouting at the sheep, kicking them, beating them over the heads with their hats, and cursing fluently, while the Reverend Sledge still watched, stony-faced.

Ferguson looked at the sheep huddled, bleating, on the dock, and said to the two boys approaching: "Close up slowly and see if you can push them toward the opening."

They got the sheep to the edge of the ferry. One animal put her foot on the deck, but at that moment one of the boys below, after wrestling with a sheep, picked it up and dropped it back into the water, creating a wave that made the ferry lurch, and the lead sheep leaped back and dived headfirst into those behind her. They resisted for a moment, then suddenly reversed themselves in their tracks and ran back to dry land.

Ferguson worked hard for four hours without getting a single sheep on board except those he carried on bodily. By noon he had a nucleus of a dozen bleating sheep on the ferry, but they all had to be tied, for the first ones had gone over or through the ropes and landed in the river.

Teddy Root took off his droopy hat and wiped the sweat from his forehead with a blue bandanna. "We ain't gettin' very far, Mr. Ferguson."

Ferguson drew a deep breath. "We aren't getting anywhere," he said. "Those sheep we carried on board haven't missed a bleat since we put them there, and I wonder if they are scaring off the others. Let's stop and eat."

Mawson stopped them. "When are you going to get started?"

Ferguson lifted his eyebrows. "They're your sheep. They aren't telling me anything."

"You're running the ferry."

"Maybe you would like to pay me for my time, and swim them across."

"No, sir, you made a deal," said Mawson. "These critters are going across on the ferry if it takes a month."

Ferguson looked at him. "Do I get the feeling that you wish it *would* take a month?"

"I have no idea what feeling you are getting."

They went to the shed — nothing more than a sod roof on poles — where Root slept and kept his few belongings. He got a piece of meat, wrapped in a dishtowel, out of a stoneware jar set partly in the water. He sniffed it and said, "Still good. The cornbread's in that tow-sack hangin' from the ridgepole." He unwrapped the meat on his blanket, and got a big jackknife out of his pocket. "Sure is hard to keep meat around here. Last night a 'coon knocked the lid off and drug the whole thing out and almost got away with it, but I hit him with a rock and he left it lay."

"It's darn good meat, too," said Ferguson, swallowing a half-chewed bite. "You're a good cook, Mr. Root."

By the time they were through, Ferguson had decided his next move. "I'm going across," he said, "to have a talk with Mr. Benson. It may be we can figure something out."

"Want me to keep on tryin'?"

"Do your best. If you get them started, all the better."

He went back to get the sorrel, and Mawson confronted him. "Givin' up?"

"What if I am?"

"You'll never take this ferry across the river until you get my sheep on it."

"Maybe you'd like to do it yourself."

"I'll buy the ferry from you. How much do you want for it?"

128

Ferguson was warned by the quickness with which Mawson had seized on an idle remark. "I will serve notice when I get ready to sell."

"I will buy it — if the price is right."

"Others have spoken ahead of you."

"Never mind them. You'll have to negotiate with me before you get through."

"Is it your idea that I can't sell where I want to?"

"It's my idea," said Mawson, "that I'm the only one who has the cash to buy you out."

Ferguson studied him. "How long have you owned these sheep?" he asked.

"Long enough," said Mawson.

"Did you buy them just to cause trouble at the ferry?"

Mawson seemed amused. "They told me you was a smart feller."

Ferguson saddled the sorrel and rode again into the stream. He came out on the Nebraska side a few feet from Yeakel and Logan. Yeakel said cheerfully, "Trouble, Ferguson?"

"I never have anything else when you're around."

Yeakel pretended astonishment. "I never had trouble with sheep."

Ferguson looked at him. "If you cut the ferry-rope last night, Yeakel, take warning; the man who cuts my rope again may find his ax against his own throat."

"Big talk, Ferguson," said Charlie Logan,

"but we got more important business — about that Injun workin' for you."

"Why are you after No Horse?"

"To save trouble," said Logan. "One of these here emigrants might take a shot at No Horse and set off an Injun war."

Ferguson said, "No Horse is a good man on the ferry."

Yeakel said, "Teddy Root runs his side by himself."

"Teddy Root gets lots of help from the emigrants who hope to speed up their turn. And Mr. Root is younger than Mr. Benson."

"Nevertheless, Ferguson," said Yeakel, "the least you can do is send No Horse back to his tribe. He has been heard making threats against our women, and we won't stand for no redskin to even think about such things."

Ferguson hesitated. "Who heard him make those threats?" he asked.

"It was told me confidentially," said Yeakel, staring at him.

Ferguson looked up to the top of the slope. No Horse stood there, watching them — a lonely figure in moccasins and woolen trousers; his bronze skin and his straight black hair would have marked him anywhere — and he knew they were talking about him. Ferguson turned back. "I don't believe it. He has a wife and two babies in Walking Bird's band, and he is honest and hard-working." He started to turn away. "When you get some honest evidence against him, tell me what it is. Meantime, I will not let anybody take advantage of him just because he is an Indian."

He walked with Benson out on the dock. "Do you know anything about sheep?"

Benson scratched his whiskered chin. "Well, now, Mr. Ferguson, I know some good things about 'em; them I can tell in a minute. I know some bad things about 'em, and them would take me all day and half the night."

"Good or bad, I want just one thing: how to get them on board the ferry."

"You need a Judas goat."

"The worst way."

"You recall a feller come through here a while back in a prairie wagon? Had a bunch of kids, two milch cows, some chickens and ducks, half a dozen pigs, and ten sheep?"

"I think I would remember any outfit like that — but I don't."

"You might not of been here. Anyway, that feller had a black-faced goat he claimed was a Judas goat that would lead sheep anywhere."

"He must be halfway to Oregon by now."

"Nope, I heard yesterday that he bought himself a claim up near the Forks. Seems his wife was about to have a baby, and he was scared to deliver it hisself because the last one came out butt first and gave him a lot of trouble."

"So he decided to settle down near Doc Doddridge," said Ferguson.

"He gave some feller fifty dollars for a quit-claim deed."

"If he has a Judas goat, get him down here. You go up by Turner's and send Obie down here to help No Horse with the ferry. These man won't bother anyone so long as somebody is looking."

"Want me to take a look-in at Noah?"

"Sally will take care of him. You get that Judas goat down here before we have a riot on the other side."

CHAPTER X

FERGUSON FOUND A soft place in the grass near the dock, and lay down with his head on the saddle, while the sorrel grazed down stream; the horse would not go far. He was asleep by the time he got his long legs stretched out, and then Obie was calling his name and touching his shoulder. "Mr. Ferguson, you want me to do anything?"

Ferguson shook his head vigorously and got his eyes open. "Just keep an eye on things. Noah all right?"

"He was at noon. Here, Mr. Ferguson." He set down a bucket covered with a clean cloth. "There's sandwiches — buff'lo meat and light-bread. We heard you was on the other side all morning fixing the ferry, and Sally thought you might not have had any chance to eat."

Ferguson sat up straight. "Your sister Sally is a rare jewel," he said. "I am starving."

"Yes, sir," said Obie. "She's nice, too."

Ferguson ate ravenously, and at the same time made fresh coffee. "Anything happening at the road ranch?"

"Not much, I guess. People talkin' about the meeting tonight."

"What meeting?"

"To organize a claim club."

"That's right, It *is* tonight. Good thing you reminded me."

"Obie," he said, "there's a pile of wood we use to build a fire on a real dark night, so the people can see in order to get off. You can grab the ax there and chop it into two-foot lengths, and just act busy and let people know you are here, so people won't bother things."

"You mean so people won't cut the rope again?"

Ferguson nodded and lay back down to sleep. The next time he woke up, it was to the blatting of a goat; he opened his eyes, and there was Benson coming up on his mule, leading at the end of a rope a black-and-white goat that protested every step of the way. "I got him, Mr. Ferguson," the old man said proudly.

"It's a her," said Ferguson, "but it makes no difference, if that goat will just lead those sheep onto the ferry. I wonder if she will swim."

"He never said."

"How much did he want for her?"

"I rented her for two dollars a day. He said that was his reg'lar price."

"If she does the work, she will be worth it." Ferguson rubbed his eyes. He felt pretty good after his nap. "Did anybody holler from the other side?" he asked Obie.

"No, sir. Lots of hollerin' went on, but not to us."

"You finished the wood?"

"Yes, sir."

Ferguson looked at the sun, and judged it to be about three o'clock. "You'd better go look in on Noah."

"Yes, sir."

"But catch up the sorrel first."

He watched activities on the other side. Apparently they were still trying, but not very hard, and he figured that bunch of sheep had been so thoroughly scared that they would not go aboard the ferry for a week.

He rode out into the water, pulling the goat behind him. At first she tried to hold back, but when the rope pulled her head down, she quit balking and began to swim like a veteran.

He rode out on the other shore, and the goat followed. Mawson was waiting for him. "What you got there?" he asked.

"A Judas goat."

"What do goats have to do with sheep?" Mawson demanded.

"A Judas goat will go where you want it to go, and the sheep will follow it," said Ferguson. "Have your boys bring up a fresh band, and we'll give them a try." He studied a train of three wagons going north out of the valley. "What's that?" he asked Teddy Root.

Root shrugged helplessly. "They had a meeting, Mr. Ferguson, and some of 'em decided to go up north and try to find a ford."

"They won't find a ford for two thousand miles."

"Then they're figuring on building a ferry of their own."

"If this keeps up," said Mawson, "pretty soon you will have nothing but a ferry for sheep. The price of your ferry just dropped a hundred dollars, and I figure another hundred for every three wagons that pull out."

Ferguson turned on him. "Mawson, are you trying to ruin my ferry?"

Mawson's sardonic eyes became calculating. "I'll get it, one way or another."

"There is no chance of that."

"You'll never move these sheep across on that ferry, but I will keep them here until you do."

It seemed obvious that Mawson had deliberately moved his sheep into position to force Ferguson out of the picture; his reason was not apparent, but might be guessed.

"I expect to move your sheep," Ferguson said.

Mawson said, "I hear you're a gambler."

"Any man who comes west is a gambler, the way I figure it."

"I'll make you a gamble," said Mawson. "Double the ferriage for the sheep, against the ferry itself, that you can't move them in three days."

Ferguson looked at him. "Make it four days."

"No. Three days from this morning."

"Today is over half gone," said Ferguson. "Three days from tomorrow morning."

He watched the avaricious gleam in Mawson's eyes, and knew he could make a bet.

"All right," Mawson said finally. "Three days from tomorrow morning."

"With a qualification," said Ferguson. "I will move them any way I can."

"And have you drown my whole outfit!"

Ferguson said carefully: "If there is any loss, I will pay the market price, to come out of my charges. If there should be more than that, I will pay it in cash."

He saw the calculating look in Mawson's eyes, and knew something was about to come. Mawson said, "I will accept that on one condition: if you move the sheep but the loss is more than your charges, I will have an interest in the ferry."

Ferguson thought about it, watching the faces of the emigrants. Mawson's black eyes, Teddy Root's puzzled expression. Ferguson had no intention of losing any substantial number of sheep. The ferry charges would be $960, and twice that would be almost two thousand dollars — a small fortune. Likewise, here was a chance to get rid of Mawson, one way or another. Mawson would be after him until he should win or until he should be convinced that he could not win. Ferguson knew that he was running some risk of losing the ferry, but he did not think it likely, for he had reserves that Mawson knew nothing about. He looked at Mawson and said, "I will accept that condition. You heard it all, Mr. Root?"

"Yes, sir. You're gamblin' the ferry against

twice the charges that you can move them sheep in three days without losin' very many of 'em."

"All right. Mawson?"

Mawson drew a great breath. "How much do you value the ferry — if I get an interest in it?"

"One thousand dollars."

"All right, Ferguson." He turned and went toward the approaching band of sheep.

Ferguson said, "Mr. Root, take the goat to meet them. Let her mingle with them; then start her off this way and we'll find out if she can lead."

Root went off toward the sheep, the goat following docilely. Ferguson turned to Sledge and two other men who had come up beside Sledge. "I hope you gentlemen realize that I am trying to make things better for you."

Sledge said, "I believe you are, Brother Ferguson. Otherwise there would be no call for you to risk your ferry. New wagons come across the prairie every day."

"I will admit that I don't like Mawson."

"You don't look to me like a man who would go out of his way to do something for somebody you don't like."

"There's more than that," said Ferguson. "That man is a troublemaker, he will cause difficulties for every emigrant here. He's a bully, and I don't like bullies — but I guess it's more than that, reverend. I came out here like everybody else; because this is a new country and a chance for everybody to start over. It ought to be a free country, so those who take the risks, who bring their wives and children through the heat and the storms and the Indians, will have a fair chance. Then some feller like Mawson comes along. . . . I admit I am going to get a great satisfaction out of getting rid of him."

"You will have him on the other side of the river when you do."

Ferguson grinned. "It's seven hundred feet closer to the Pacific Ocean."

"I admire your courage, Mr. Ferguson," said Sledge, "and I will help all I can. All of us here will stay at least until the time is up, and we will try to persuade the other emigrants to stay too." He turned to the men with him. "Agreed?"

They nodded, and one man spoke vehemently: "I hope you beat him, Mr. Ferguson."

"I am going to try," said Ferguson.

"I don't think there's any point in leaving anyway," said one of the men. "Down by Omaha City you have to wait a week, and up above there ain't no ferry — and I don't trust this here river. They tell me she can rise in an hour till a man can't cross her in a boat even."

Ferguson agreed. "It's a dangerous river. A man could lose his wagon and team and all his family if he doesn't know the water."

"Brother Mawson is bringing another band of sheep," said Sledge.

Ferguson went out to meet them, and found that Root had put the goat into the band, and the goat was now stepping out in front as if she knew what was wanted; the sheep plodded along behind as if they had been following the goat all their lives, and Ferguson felt relieved.

The goat led the way up the wooden dock. Ferguson stepped alongside her at the last moment, took her collar, and steered her onto the ferry. The sheep followed without a second look.

When they were all on, Root closed the opening with the rope, and Ferguson called across the river: "All right, Mr. Benson." Then he said, "Mr. Root, we might as well take the goat off. We can use her to bring down the next bunch, and be ready for the ferry again." He turned to Mawson, whose black eyes were glinting, and Ferguson knew definitely that Mawson was not pleased. "Cut a hundred and eighty next time," Ferguson said. "We can speed it up a little."

"You'll crowd 'em too much, and they'll push each other off the ferry."

"My risk," said Ferguson. "Bring a hundred and eighty."

Root picked up the goat in his arms and carried her, blatting and struggling, off the ferry and set her on the dock. The ferry began to move away slowly as Benson's team got into the collars.

"You reckon one of us oughta go with them?" asked Root.

"I'll go," said Ferguson. "Mr. Benson might have trouble getting them off the ferry." He

140

turned to Mawson. "You'd better send a couple of your boys over, too. I'm not responsible for them once they are on dry land."

Mawson turned to his four sons and nodded. Two of them ran lumbering to the ferry, and got on. Ferguson jumped the gap at the last moment, and settled down for the slow but steady movement across the brown water. He looked at the two boys — as tall as Ferguson and much heavier. "Which two are you?" he asked.

"I'm Dutch," said the older one. "He's Matt."

"You people haven't had these sheep long," Ferguson suggested.

"Long enough," said Dutch.

"You aren't sheepmen, though."

"We was miners," said the younger one. "Pa owned a coal mine in Pennsylvania."

"Shut up!" Dutch growled.

Matt looked at him resentfully. "You ain't runnin' me."

"Pa told you not to tell him nothin'."

Matt glowered, but he refused to say any more. However, Ferguson had learned all he needed to know for the moment; that Zachariah Mawson was not a sheepman, that he had only recently bought the 12,000 sheep, and that undoubtedly his only motive had not been to take them west. However, sheep in the west should be money-makers, and for the time being, at least, Mawson could take that outfit to Kearney or somewhere along the Oregon

Trail, and sell them off as mutton to the emigrants for twice what they had cost him.

Obviously, also, Mawson had had his eye on the ferry all the time; perhaps he had heard of it by prairie-dog telegraph; perhaps, even, he had been put up to it by Yeakel or Logan.

One thing was sure, Ferguson decided as the ferry neared the Nebraska shore: all this was not accidental. The coming of Mawson, the colored lithographs with the non-existent townsite, the attempts to buy the ferry — all these were part of a master plan. But who was behind it? Was it Major Yeakel, Charlie Logan, or Simmons? Or even Wiggins?

The ferry nosed into the water at the north side of the dock, and Ferguson noted that Benson had measured the length of rope well, for he had stopped the mules at exactly the right time. He picked up the small coil of rope at the stern and leaped onto the dock, threw a half-hitch around the snubbing-post, and put some pressure on it. The ferry slowed down and swung out a little at the bow, then settled in against the dock under the pressure of the current. Benson, having stopped the mules and thrown the rope off the double-tree, was hurrying back to the dock, but before he reached it, Ferguson had made fast the stern rope and was pulling up the long rope that went to the snubbing-post on shore and acted as an anchor.

"It looks like the feller's goat did the trick," said Benson. "I figured we could get them off

142

by ourselves," said Ferguson.

"Be strange if we can't. You want me to get No Horse down here to help?"

Ferguson looked at the two sullen young men in the black hats. "I think not. Let No Horse stay up there. We're going to have enough trouble just trying to keep him *out* of trouble."

When the ferry was snug against the dock, they took down the ropes on that side, and Ferguson waited for the sheep to move.

But nothing happened. One or two sheep approached the edge but drew back.

"They don't like the crack," said Benson.

"Or worse," said Ferguson. "They like the ferry too much to leave it."

Dutch Mawson grabbed his big hat and gave a shout. His younger brother followed his example. They both rushed at the sheep to force them onto the dock, but the sheep, frightened, crowded into the far end of the ferry, bleating helplessly. Ferguson seized Dutch Mawson by the shoulder and spun him. "Leave those sheep alone," he said.

"We was helpin'."

"You don't have to do anything until the sheep get on dry land. Then they're yours."

Dutch began to glower. "You put your hands on me again, and I'll whup you."

"You interfere with my work again," said Ferguson coldly, and I'll hit you so hard you'll come down in Omaha City."

Dutch rushed at him, but Ferguson slid to

143

one side and kept out of range. He led the man onto the dock, got him against the far side, and then waded in and hammered at Dutch's face until Dutch gave way. Then Ferguson bored in with a hard hammering of fists to the man's chin, and Dutch, backing from the attack, stepped off the edge of the dock and went into the water.

Ferguson went back to the boat.

"Mister," said Matt, "our pa will fix you for that."

Ferguson merely glanced at him. "You'd better go help your brother out of the mud," he said. "We have sheep to unload, and we don't want interference, so you and your brother keep busy at something that won't get you into trouble."

Matt left, and Ferguson said, "Mr. Benson, let's carry a couple of these critters off the boat."

They got two of the sheep in their arms, and set them on the dock. The sheep stood for a moment, bleating, then dashed back onto the ferry, and all the sheep on the barge crowded back against the ropes, bleating in panic. Ferguson took a deep breath.

"Maybe you'll have to get the goat," said Benson.

"It doesn't make any sense at all," said Ferguson. He looked up suddenly. "Wait a minute."

Dutch and Matt started to walk out on the

dock, but Ferguson went to meet them. "If you interfere," he said. "I will call the whole thing off. I will shut down the ferry until your pa moves his sheep away."

"You can't," said Dutch.

Ferguson smiled in satisfaction. "If the ferry doesn't run for a week, what happens to your pa's sheep?"

"Nothin'," said Dutch.

"Plenty," said Ferguson.

"Nothin' can happen. We'll keep 'em there until we get control of the ferry."

Ferguson smiled. So that really was the object of the whole thing. He said, "You are not going to get control of the ferry, for while you are waiting, your sheep have to eat, and in another twelve hours they will have eaten every blade of grass within miles."

They stared at him, and at that moment, some distance beyond them, Yeakel and Logan rode into sight on the slope and started down.

"It's worth thinking about," said Ferguson. "Three days is about as long as you can keep those sheep within any distance of the dock on the Iowa side. Then they will start to die."

"Pa never said that."

"Maybe he didn't think about it, but I am telling you now, those sheep have to eat or they will die off, so the best thing you can do is go up there on the slope and wait till we get this load off the ferry."

They were puzzled, but they could not fail to

recognize the validity of his argument. Finally Dutch said, "Let's go," and they both left the dock.

Ferguson said, "Come on, Mr. Benson, let's go make some coffee."

"Sounds good," said Benson, "but what about the woolies?"

"Give them a chance to settle down."

"All right." He felt in his pocket for a chew. "We run out of wood, and I sent Obie out with his pa's team to get us a load of buffalo-chips."

Ferguson nodded. "Anything to eat?"

"Sally Turner sent over a pan of real good cornbread."

Benson looked up. "You reckon them two fellers are goin' to try to throw a scare into the sheep?"

Ferguson looked at Yeakel and Logan. "I doubt it. They —"

He stopped. Yeakel and Logan had gone straight to Dutch and Matt Mawson, and had started to converse in low tones without any apparent introduction. Ferguson said to Benson, "When is the last time those two crossed the river?"

" 'Bout a week ago — on the ferry."

Ferguson got to his feet.

Benson said, "They're headin' for No Horse."

Ferguson ran up the slope, but reached the Indian too late. Logan was reading him the riot act. "You're a damn' no-good Indian," he said, "and we're servin' notice: you get the hell out

146

of here fast. We don't want no Indians in this part of the country."

No Horse watched him impassively, but said, "Mr. Logan, I'm not doing anything but helping Mr. Ferguson with the ferry."

"Takin' a job away from a good, honest American."

Ferguson reached him. He seized Logan's shoulder and spun him around hard, down the slope, so that Logan floundered for a moment and then went on his face in the dust.

Yeakel said harshly, "Ferguson, you are going to do that once too often."

Ferguson said, "Keep your hands off of that pistol. And stay away from my helper. I need No Horse to work with the ferry — but you don't want me to operate the ferry. Further, you picked on an innocent Indian who was American long before you were." He watched Logan get out of the dirt.

"You can't play God just because you run the ferry," said Logan bitterly.

A folded newspaper had dropped from Logan's hand, but he did not pick it up. "If you know the Mawsons, get on down there and help them with their sheep," said Ferguson.

Logan's eyes were baleful. "You won't last, Ferguson. I'll see to that."

Ferguson waited until they walked away, then said to No Horse: "You scared?"

The Indian, hardly eighteen, looked after the two men and moistened his lips. "I don't know,

147

Mr. Ferguson. They are bad men, but they don't fight in the open. I think they are after me."

"Any reason why?"

No Horse looked at him. "Mr. Logan was across the river a couple weeks ago, tried to buy my sister for one night. I said no. He was drunk, and we had to put him out of the village."

For the first time, Ferguson felt discouraged. He wondered if there were too many things for him to cope with. He said, "Don't do anything hasty, No Horse, but if you think it is best, stay with your people. You're a good worker, and I'd like to keep you, but I don't want you to get into a fight you can't win."

The young Indian regarded him solemnly. "Thank you, Mr. Ferguson. Most people say Indian no-good worker."

"I don't," Ferguson said warmly. "If it gets too much for you, you can get your money from me or Mr. Benson any time."

"I will think about it — and talk to Walking Bird. He is a wise man."

"Fine." Ferguson went back down the slope, keeping an eye on the two men, who were now talking to the two Mawsons. "They've sure got their minds set on making trouble, haven't they?"

"It looks that way," said Benson, pouring coffee into tin cups. "Mr. Ferguson, I'm worried. You got all them sheep to get across the river, and you got all these skunks tryin' to keep you from it."

Ferguson looked at him. "I guess you're right. Do you think they can do it?"

Benson bit off a mouthful of cornbread, and said after a minute: "I got lots of respect for you, Mr. Ferguson, but you sure got the short end of the stick."

"Sort of like fighting with your hands tied under your knees."

Ferguson got to his feet. "One sheep has just walked across the crack, and others are starting to follow. That part of our problem is about to be solved."

"But you can't go somewhere to have dinner between every boatload."

"That's obvious." He studied the four men, who were watching the sheep begin to pour out onto the dock. "There are twelve thousand to be moved in three days."

"You couldn't move that many even if everything was going right — which it ain't."

Ferguson nodded. "We'll have to keep trying, though."

"If you try to swim 'em, it might be worse because the river might come up."

"They're heading toward shore now," said Ferguson. "In a minute we can saunter over and get behind them."

The four watching men stayed quiet while Ferguson and Benson herded the sheep to the left. Then Ferguson said to Dutch Mawson,

"They're yours now. Think you can handle them?"

Dutch did not answer.

Benson chuckled. "He looks as if he'd just et a green persimmon. Hey, what's the matter with No Horse?"

The Indian was running down the slope waving a paper. "Mr. Ferguson!" He unfolded the paper. "This is the *Chronicle*, Mr. Ferguson, and there is an editorial about you."

Ferguson saw that the date was of that day, and read from the left-hand column on the front page:

"*Who said there was no God in Nebraska?* Those who doubt it, are invited to attend the landing of Ferguson's ferry any morning about sunrise, to observe the great man make decisions for the benefit of his own personal likes and dislikes. The next few days are expected, however, for it is rumored that divinity will be occupied solving a problem the subjects of which pay no attention to his arbitrary dicta.

"It is rumored also that His Divine Excellence will call a meeting tonight to organize a claim club. As any such organization is strictly illegal and a violation of law, we urge all who believe in the process of constitutionality to stay away from said meeting and show this flaunter of the law that Nebraska will have none of his tyrannical ilk."

Ferguson looked at No Horse. "He has taken a stand, anyway."

150

No Horse said, "He is a man with the brain of a mouse."

"He wants what he wants," said Ferguson, and went back to the ferry. "All right, Mr. Root," he called. "Pull her back."

He cast off the ropes, and Benson got ready to ease off the towrope. The ferry began to move, and, even in the face of the problem facing him, Ferguson felt better because they had taken the first step. It was five o'clock in the afternoon, and they could go at it until midnight; he could hire some of the emigrants to help him, and that would speed things up and also keep the emigrants from rebelling. The ferry was sliding alongside the dock, and Ferguson said: "It looks good, Mr. Benson."

"Not too good yet," said Benson, "but better than this mornin'."

"Mr. Ferguson! Mr. Ferguson!" It was a faint cry from far away, and Ferguson looked up toward the slope.

Obie Turner was coming down, drumming his bare heels against the sides of a mule. "Mr. Ferguson! You better get home quick!"

Ferguson leaped from the ferry as it parted from the dock, and ran to meet Obie. "What's the trouble — Noah?" he asked, holding the mule's mane.

"No, sir. Not Noah. He's all right, but somebody has just drove a herd of hogs onto your south quarter."

"Hogs?"

"Yes, sir. Me and Noah counted 'em. Two hundred and four head."

Benson said, "Mr. Ferguson, they're out to ruin your land. Them hogs will root up everything."

"Not only ruin it," Ferguson said slowly, "but also confiscate it." He looked up at Obie. "You stay here, son, and help Mr. Benson. I'll take your mule back to see what's up."

CHAPTER XI

FERGUSON STOPPED AT the tavern to see Tom Turner. "What do you know about these hogs?" he asked.

"Not much." Turner waddled over to the beer barrel. "Obie saw 'em over there this afternoon when he went to look in on Noah." He drew a tin cup full of beer. "A few minutes ago some fellers were here and said the hogs belonged to Simmons."

"Simmons? I never knew he had hogs."

"I reckon he's got 'em now."

"Where's Noah?"

"He's workin' in the well."

"I'll send him home, and then I'll see about the hogs."

"You better not go startin' a fight. They tell me Simmons has got three killers waitin' for you."

Ferguson said grimly, "That doesn't stop me from ordering him off my land."

"It might get you pretty badly bunged up, though."

"I'll watch that," said Ferguson.

"It'd be a heap better if you was to wait till the claim club gets organized tonight."

"Then it would look as if I wanted the claim club organized for my own benefit." He got up. "I think I'd better go along. It's nearing supper-time, and I'm looking forward to some of Sally's buffalo roast."

Tom Turner seemed concerned. "Don't git yourself into somethin' you can't stop."

Ferguson said, "I'll tell you how it comes out. It might be just a mistake."

He rode to his cabin and tied the mule at the well. He started to call down the well to Noah, but heard sounds from the cabin, and went to investigate. The back door was open, and inside was Sally Turner, with bare feet and in her thin dress, pounding a square nail above the tiny window. He looked at the other window and saw a white curtain there. She was aware of him by that time, and turned to speak to him, but she was standing on a stump, and in turning she stepped on the edge and started to fall. He leaped to catch her, and reached her just as she started over, arms flying. The stump went back against the wall, and Sally went forward into his arms.

He held her for a moment, getting the feel of her — and it was good. Then he looked into her eyes, as blue as a butterfly's wing, and, gradually but irrevocably, he lowered his head and kissed her.

She didn't giggle, as he had half expected her to do. Her eyes opened wider, and she stared deep into his as if her soul was bared to him, with nothing held back. He kissed her again, and her arms went around his neck, and she clung to him so tightly it seemed that he might never get loose. And he didn't think he wanted to. He kissed her once more and let her down gently. She looked at him with the complete confidence that meant to him that she was in love.

"I always wondered what kissin' was about," she said wonderingly. "Now I know." She threw her arms around him and kissed him again, and he responded in spite of thinking that he should not. Then he drew back.

He said gently, "We'd better see about Noah."

She said, "I'll finish poundin' in my nail, and then your curtains will be up."

"I'll see you outside, Sally."

He was just going through the door when she called to him. "Mr. Ferguson!"

"Yes?"

"Do you think I can cook good?"

He went back and looked down at her. "You are the best cook in Nebraska territory," he told her. In spite of himself he kissed her once more, and then left in a hurry. He went to the well and leaned over to call Noah. "You all right?"

The muffled answer came back presently: "All right, Mr. Ferguson. You're early, ain't you?"

"A little — but come on up. That's enough for today."

"I better send some dirt up first."

"Save it for tomorrow."

155

"All right. Hoist away."

He tied the well-rope to the saddlehorn and rode the mule north until the bucket appeared, and Noah climbed out, put the bucket on the curb, and began to dust his overalls.

Sally came out and said, "The curtains are all up now, Mr. Ferguson."

He smiled at her. "I'm obliged to you."

"You're welcome." She went to the corral, where her bareback horse was playfully tossing straw. She bridled the horse and led him outside. For a moment the sun was behind her; then she mounted the horse by use of the fence, with her dress above her bare knees.

He stopped her as she rode out. "Miss Sally," he said, "You're a big girl. You need to wear something under your dress."

She grinned knowingly. "You don't like me this way, Mr. Ferguson?"

"I do," he said. "What's worrying me is that others will see you that way too, and they will talk."

She giggled, then suddenly slammed her heels into the horse's sides and galloped off.

Ferguson asked Noah: "How deep are you now?"

"Two twenty-two, the way I figure — and some show of water, but I don't think it will amount to anything."

"I wouldn't expect it to, at that depth."

Noah wrinkled his nose. "Pigs!" he said.

"Yes, just over the rise there, I guess."

"Whose?"

"I'm not sure."

"Hey!" said Noah. "That's your land, over the ridge."

"Yes."

"And you don't know whose pigs are on it?"

"Not yet."

"You better be findin' out."

"That's where I'm going now."

"I'll go with you."

"You'll do nothing of the kind." Ferguson smiled at the dirt-covered boy; he was a small boy for his age, but full of vinegar. "This might turn out to be a lot of trouble, and I won't be responsible to your pa if something happens to you."

"I better go get help, then."

"That's not a bad idea."

"But don't start nothin' till I get back." He climbed onto the mule. "If there's gonna be a fight, I want to see it at the beginning."

Ferguson grinned. "I'll do my best."

He stood for a moment, then walked up the easy slope to the top of the rise.

From under a tree rose Simmons.

"Your hogs?" asked Ferguson pleasantly.

Simmons said guardedly, "Yes."

"Red Durocs — they will make nice bacon."

Simmons nodded, watching.

"You're on my land without permission," said Ferguson.

"How much land you got?"

"Three hundred and twenty."

"That's twice what the gover'ment allows."

Ferguson knew what the argument would be now, but he said, "It is allowed by the territorial legislature."

"But it ain't been surveyed and it can't be recorded until the U.S. land office opens up for business."

Ferguson said quietly, "Mr. Simmons, I preempted this land when there was nothing and nobody on it. It was legal to claim three hundred and twenty, and I took it, as did many others at that time."

"I got no land," said Simmons, walking closer.

"You did not get here early enough."

Simmons stopped. "I figure you got more than you are entitled to, so I might as well have this quarter."

Ferguson said, "I will throw you off, and if your hogs are still here by dark, I will have ham and bacon for next winter."

"I reckon not," said a familiar voice behind him, and he turned to the giant figure of Zachariah Mawson, flanked by the two boys who had been on the other side of the river.

Ferguson said, "It looks as if you have brought enough help to try to whip me."

"I don't need help," Mawson growled.

"But you brought it."

Mawson asked ominously, "What was that

remark about ham and bacon next winter?"

"From the way you have left your sheep, you must be trying to furnish mutton for somebody. You're supposed to be loading them."

"I never agreed to help."

"How did you know Simmons?" asked Ferguson.

"That's our personal affair."

"You knew him, and you knew where to find him," Ferguson said. "It was sheep, and now it's hogs." Ferguson took a step forward. "Since you've got me cut out for the slaughter, I might as well get in first lick." He launched himself at Mawson, and caught him off-guard. Ferguson's long arms flashed in and out, up and down, and for a moment he had the advantage. Mawson began to topple like a felled tree, and Ferguson hit him with his full power to put him down.

Mawson stumbled back and rallied. But Ferguson was on him again. Mawson straightened, looked dazed for a moment; then Ferguson lashed into him with all his fury, and Mawson, his eyes glazed, turned his feet to run, but then tripped himself and went down on his face, heavily.

The boys came to life then, and rushed him both at once. Ferguson backed up and tried to keep them off, but one or the other caught him with great, hamlike fists that drove him back. He saw Mawson get to his knees and shake his head like a big bear, then get to his feet, and by that time, Mawson's black eyes had regained all their cunning calculation. He said, "Hold him, boys. This is one squatter we'll teach to have respect for us." Ferguson took his last good shot at the man, but it was futile. He could not get past the big man's arms, and Mawson kept coming in toward him; Ferguson had to back up.

He found himself in a bear-hug from the back, and Mawson stepped in and began to slug him in the face. He raised both legs and slammed him in the stomach, and Mawson grunted but kept coming. Ferguson raised his legs again, and the man holding him let him drop, and kicked him as he rolled over to get in the clear.

He knew he was scheduled for a slaughter, but there was nothing he could do. He got to his feet and started to straighten up when one of them kicked him from behind and put him back on his face.

He rolled again, to avoid those cowhide-booted legs, but they were waiting for him, and he rolled against Simmons' legs and found himself stopped. He seized the man's legs and threw his weight against them, and Simmons fell heavily. Ferguson bounded to his feet, but the Mawsons were ready for him. Again he was bear-hugged from behind, and Mawson, his black eyes cold with fury, stepped into him and began to throw those pile-driver fists into Ferguson's face and against his jaw. Ferguson felt them hit; he felt his head snap back each time;

he heard the crack of bone against bone; and finally he went limp. The last he knew was that the big man hit him again, and his head rolled on a limp neck. He knew vaguely that blood was running down his face, and then he dropped, and everything went black when they began to kick him.

CHAPTER XII

HE CAME TO as water was being squeezed over his face, and looked up at the dark eyes and white skin of Mrs. Talbot, who was shaking her head. "Terrible!" she said. "Who could do a thing like this?"

He closed his eyes and took a deep breath, and it helped a little. She continued to put water on his face, and then very gently to sponge off the blood and dirt, crooning like a mother over a sick child.

"You came along at a good time," he said through swollen and puffy lips.

She helped him sit up, and he saw tears in her eyes. "It's terrible," she said.

"How did you find me?" he asked.

Her hands were very gentle as she continued to bathe his face from a wooden bucket of water. "I heard the shouts, and saw men gathered around something on the ground, and I thought it was a dog-fight. But they left, and I came to see, never dreaming — I saw it was a man, and ran back for water. Then I came and found you!"

He got to his feet, shaking his head to clear it, and leaned heavily on her. They walked across the field to her cabin, and by that time he was walking by himself, but his body felt bruised all over, and his face was a great mass of raw meat and aching flesh. He went into her cabin, ducking his head to keep from bumping the door frame, and sat down on a stump in a corner. He leaned back wearily. "I don't think I've ever been so tired."

"No wonder." She said, "I'm going to bathe your face in buttermilk. It will sting a little, but it will take out the soreness."

"All right, ma'am."

"Here's hot coffee."

"Thank you."

"But be careful. Your lips are cut and bruised."

He nodded. "I'll wait till it cools a little."

"Now come over to the table here and let me work on you."

She bustled around him, and he inhaled deeply the faint fragrance of perfume. He said, "It was sure nice of you to pick me up out of the dirt."

She turned to him, tears again in her eyes. "It was brutal! They were like wild animals!"

"They're going to be surprised when they find out they have to do it all over again."

She said, shaking her head, "you're not going to fight with them *again!*"

"I have to whip them or get out of the country. And I'm not getting out. I came here when the land was open, and I got what I was entitled to."

She said slowly, "You could be forgiven for killing the men who treated you like that."

"I'm not a killing man," he said, "unless I have to be."

"They say you're a bone breaker."

"Who told you that?"

"Mr. Keller was here this morning."

He looked at her. "What's he doing around?"

"He didn't say. I think he's sort of a guard for somebody."

"I think you're right — and I know who that somebody is." He winced as she poured buttermilk over his face with a tablespoon.

"You can stay here all night," she said. "They might be waiting for you at your cabin."

"I would like to," he said, "but there's a meeting tonight to organize a claim club —"

"You can't go anywhere tonight!"

"A little whipping isn't going to lay me up for a couple of weeks," he said, feigning surprise.

"You didn't get a little whipping. You got a vicious mauling."

He said, "Ma'am, would you like a big supply of ham and bacon for next winter?"

She was puzzled. "I won't be here next winter," she said at last. "I can't stand it here alone much longer." She shuddered.

He sat back. "What are you putting on my face now?"

"I'm putting a piece of bacon on that cut the doctor sewed together. It hasn't been broken open, but —" She shook her beautiful head, and her black hair gleamed in the last light of the sun.

"And then what?" he insisted.

"Cream for the cuts and bruises. I was saving it to make butter, but you need it more than I do."

"I'll be obliged to you, Mrs. Talbot."

"I'm sure you will," she said enigmatically.

After a while, he drank the coffee as best he could, and gathered his strength to go back to his cabin.

"You have gentle hands," he said, "and beautiful hair."

She smiled wanly. He got up and put on his hat. "I'm obliged to you for everything. I'd still be out there if you hadn't come."

Suddenly she put her arms around him and hugged him, and then as suddenly stepped back; that stark look was on her face in the twilight, and she said, "Mr. Ferguson, whatever you think of me in the future, I hope you will remember me like this."

He shook his head slowly. "I could hardly remember you any other way, could I?"

He brushed her lips with his own, touched her hand, and was gone.

The tavern was crowded that night, with Tom Turner drawing beer in tin cups and coffee cups while the men kept Sally busy bringing in sandwiches. Ferguson counted forty-some men, and a few more were coming from north and south.

"Saw Injuns today," said Art Grimes, the man with the droopy-brimmed hat. "Reckon they are on the warpath."

Ferguson looked up. "There are worse things loose. This face did not come from Indians."

Grimes was silent for a moment. "They sure worked you over. Who was it?"

"Four men who were trying to take half of my land."

"Maybe they were mad at you," suggested Roy Ernest.

"They had no occasion to be mad at me — but they did want my land."

"Simmons and who else?" asked Black Gallagher.

Ferguson hesitated. "Three Mawsons."

"They musta had it in for you," Roy Ernest insisted, crossing his long, loose-jointed legs.

Ferguson said sharply, "They have nothing against me except that I have something they want. They claimed my south quarter, and took it over today."

"With them hogs?" asked Dave Ackerman. "I seen them goin' cross-country about noon, headed northwest. I thought he was leavin' the country with 'em."

"He wasn't."

"Where'd he git two hundred head of hogs?" asked scrawny Job Sye. "I never seen that many hogs over here."

"Prob'ly come up from Omaha City."

"Simmons never struck me as no hog man," said Gallagher.

"He musta had some help drivin' 'em," said Grimes.

"George Keller, that new feller come over yesterday morning," said Ackerman, and added, "Here he comes now."

The men around the table turned silent, and watched the door as Keller staggered up to it, knocked off his hat on the frame, bent down to pick it up, lost his balance and fell face forward on the floor.

"He's sure drunk," said Gallagher.

Keller got up, lurched toward an empty chair and sat down and pounded on the table. "Waiter, waiter!" he shouted.

Tom Turner waddled back to his corner. "There'll be a waiter. You want food?"

Keller shouted: "Food and whisky?"

"No whisky," said Turner.

"Beer, then."

"You're already drunk," said Turner.

"Whatsa difference? Ain't my money as good as his'n?" He pointed at Ferguson.

Tom Turner looked at him for a moment, then drew a tin cup full of beer and took it over.

"What's this you started to say about the Indians?" Ferguson asked Art Grimes.

Grimes prepared to tell his tale with relish. "They are goin' around tellin' people the land belongs to them, and they are goin' to take it back, then offer to leave it alone for ten dollars."

"Are people paying it?"

"Who wants to get massacred?" asked Grimes.

"The Indians are only a nuisance," said Ferguson. "The men we have to fight are men like Simmons."

Benson came in, looking for Ferguson. He found him and came over to sit down. "Have some beer, Mr. Benson?" asked Ferguson.

"Not right now. I'd like some coffee, though. I get tired of that stuff I make."

"You'll get it. How are things at the ferry?"

"That's what —" He peered suddenly at Ferguson's face. "Hey, you look like you been run through a coffee-grinder."

"Not all the way through," said Ferguson. "What happened at the ferry?"

"I sent the ferry back when you left this afternoon, but I ain't had no load since then, Mr. Ferguson."

He thought about it for a moment.

"Teddy Root come over, an' he says the Mawsons lit out for somewheres."

Ferguson nodded.

"An' he said you bet the ferry you could move them sheep — and you got three days from tomorrow morning."

Ackerman stared. "You bet the ferry?"

"It was the only way I could bring things to a head," said Ferguson. "His idea was to camp there and run everybody away."

"If you lose the ferry," said Ackerman in a

scared voice, "we won't have no friend anywhere. Yeakel and Logan will take over."

"I haven't lost it."

"How many sheep you got to move in two
days and three nights? Maybe we can help."

"Twelve thousand," said Ferguson.

"Jee-rusal*em!*"

"We already got a hundred and fifty across,"
said Benson, "but them fellers kep 'em so
choused up a man can't do nothin' with 'em."

Sally came in and looked at Ferguson as she
went by and smiled — an intimate little gesture
that spoke of secret things between them. She
went to Keller's table and asked: "You want
somethin', mister?"

He looked at her for a moment, and his eyes
widened. He looked her all the way up and
down, and her face turned red. Tom Turner
started over toward them. "Go back in the
kitchen, Sally. I'll take care of him."

"No, you won't!" said Keller. "Sure I want
somethin', sister. I want you!" His arm went
around her hips and he got up, raising her dress
to the middle of her bare white thighs.

Sally struggled to get away. Old Tom tried to
hurry to them. Ferguson jumped to his feet.

She beat on his chest with her doubled-up
fists, but Keller laughed. He held her tight, and
with his right hand he unbuckled his belt. She
screamed, and Ferguson leaped across the
room. He seized Keller's left arm and tore it
from around Sally. Keller paused, seeming now

169

to be cold sober. His eyes narrowed, and he told Ferguson: "You figger to do to me what you done to Jerome Talbot?"

Ferguson began to circle him. It would have to be quick and fast, for Ferguson was too bruised to take many blows. Keller turned, and Ferguson watched his feet from the corner of his eye. When he saw Keller off-balance, he stepped in, throwing long, looping blows at the man's face, maintaining a coldly furious tornado of bone-hard fists.

Keller tried to back away but couldn't. He tried to get his arms up, but it was too late. Ferguson was working on his chin with savage intensity, and Keller began to crumple. He went to the dirt floor, and Tom Turner, white as sand in the sunlight, put his foot in the middle of Keller's face and stepped on him with all the weight of his four hundred pounds.

Sally fled to the kitchen.

Dave Ackerman looked around at the men. "What are we gonna do with him?" he asked.

Art Grimes said, "He didn't really do nothin'."

Ackerman looked at him with scorn. "He tried, didn't he?"

Simon Hudson offered a suggestion: "He was drunk when he done it. He wasn't really responsible."

Black Gallagher said with fine scorn: "Well, now, Mr. Hudson, any man can get himself drunk and commit any crime he has a mind to,

170

and you would let him go free. If he acts like that when he gets drunk, he has no right to get drunk."

Dave Ackerman said, "Mr. Hudson, if a man tried to rape your daughter before a roomful of men, would you excuse him for it?"

Hudson said timorously, "Why do we have to take the law in our hands? We're in the right, aren't we? And right will prevail."

Ferguson said, "In a new country, being in the right is not enough, because there are other men in the country who don't care about the right, who know there is no law to protect their victims, and who think only of their own avaricious or perverted desires. That kind feeds on the man who thinks he is safe because he's in the right."

Hans Osterman offered his judgment: "There's sure somethin' wrong with Keller, and we don't want his kind in Nebraska. I say the sooner we dispose of him, the better off the country will be."

"You turn him loose," said Roy Ernest heatedly, "and what have you got? The next time, it'll be *your* wife, and it may be in the dark when nobody is around. I say we hang 'im!"

"Me too!" shouted a dozen men.

Dave Ackerman asked, "What do you say, Mr. Ferguson?"

"I see no excuse for this sort of conduct," said Ferguson, now more shaken than before. "The reason makes no difference; the fact is

171

that this man tried to commit the most unforgivable crime on the frontier. The only protection our women have is what we give them: the sure knowledge that any man who violates them will be punished immediately."

"Hang 'im! Hang 'im!"

Dave Ackerman started to drag Keller across the floor, but Keller recovered consciousness and tried to get to his feet.

"Wait a minute," said Ferguson. "You can't just take a man out and hang him. That's lynch law."

"What else have we got?" demanded Gallagher.

"We can have an organized body here when we form the claim club."

"That's nothin' but vigilante law, anyways," said Grimes.

"Partly," Ferguson admitted. "It has been used all over the country where the law is slow getting in, and has some legal standing. It keeps things in control until the law gets there."

Keller get to his feet. His face was bloody, and his nose was sunken in where Turner had stepped on it; he looked wildly around the room and said huskily: "You can't hang me without a trial."

Ferguson looked at him. "You will get a trial," he said.

"I was just foolin'. I never done nothin' like this before. I was just playin'."

"No man plays about things like that," said Ferguson.

"He says it's the first time," said Hudson doubtfully.

Ferguson looked at him. "Mr. Hudson, you may be so afraid of doing something wrong that you are afraid to do something right. You ought to know there is no first time for a man like him. He's been doing these things all his life."

"How do you know that?"

"I have seen many men plead first offense, and I have defended some of them — and in every case it turned out that it was not a first offense at all. These things grow, and get a little worse every time. They don't happen all of a sudden."

"Anybody got a rope handy?" asked Ackerman in a loud voice.

"Wait a minute!" said Ferguson. "Not that fast."

"Why not?"

"We will have to go through with the formality of a trial by an organized body — and we'll do it later. Not tonight. Give yourselves some time to cool off. Organize the claim club and appoint a committee to arrange the details of a trial."

"What's the use? We're gonna hang him anyway," said Gallagher.

"It keeps it from being too easy to do, and it gives an accused man some protection. When you set up the details, you want to consider it as if you are the man accused and you are innocent, and you want a fair trial. That's the only way we can give it legality."

"It's a waste of time," muttered Ackerman.

"A few hours' delay in the name of justice is not a waste of time."

"All right." Ackerman did not like it, though. "What'll we do with him in the meantime?"

"Tie him up and hang him about forty feet down the dry well across the road," said Roy Ernest. "That'll hold him till tomorrow."

All this time Keller had been silent, seeming to have sunken into a semi-stupor. Hans Osterman brought a rope, and they tied his feet, and ran the rope around his chest under his arms; then they tied his hands behind him. "There, I reckon he looks like a trussed goose," said Roy Ernest, stepping back.

"I'll say he was the handsomest feller in Nebraska," said Ackerman, "but he don't look so good now. He looks like he's just out of bed with bilious fever."

"Take him out and lower him down the well," said Ferguson. "He won't be very comfortable, but I guess it doesn't make much difference."

"We better post a guard," said Gallagher.

"He ain't goin' nowhere," said Ackerman.

"He'll be all right for a while," said Turner. "My dogs will hear it if anybody tries to get him out."

In half an hour they were back. "He tried to buy us off," said Ackerman.

"For how much?"

"He said he could get a thousand dollars by tomorrow."

Ferguson thought about it. "He doesn't know anybody here."

"He spent most of his time shinin' up to wimmen," said Gallagher.

And, Ferguson remembered, he had come over originally to make the ferry deal for Mawson. Would Mawson try to rescue him? They would have to wait to see.

CHAPTER XIII

HE LOOKED AROUND the room and ticked them off: Big Dave Ackerman, good hearted and friendly; Roy Ernest, with his long legs and double-jointed ankles; beetle-browed Black Gallagher; Art Grimes with his droopy hat; Hans Osterman; Nosey Porter; Job Sye, scrawny and nervous; Tom Turner; and thirty others. Ferguson called the meeting to order. "We first elect a temporary chairman," he said, "And I nominate Dave Ackerman."

"Second," said Grimes.

"All in favor say aye."

They voted Ackerman in unanimously, and Ackerman said, "What do I do now?"

"I will propose a constitution and by-laws. If the meeting adopts them, we can go ahead and elect officers. The president can appoint committees as provided in the by-laws, and this can be a working organization before we leave here tonight."

Grimes said dubiously, "We ain't in that big a hurry, are we?"

"If you're not in a hurry," said Ferguson, "you'd better not organize at all, because these highbinders are already here."

"You got the constitution and by-laws?" asked Ackerman.

"I have some to suggest." He stood up. "If

176

you gentlemen will bear with me for a while —" he began. "We will have to have a name first."

"I move we call it the Ferguson's Ferry Protective Claim Association," said Roy Ernest.

A general vote of aye.

Ferguson pulled a notebook from his pocket and began to read: "Constitution and by-laws adopted this blank day of June, 1859, at a meeting of the citizens of the Ferguson's Ferry community and its environs.

"Whereas it sometimes becomes necessary for persons to associate themselves together for the purpose of protecting their lives and property, their having left the peaceful shades of civilization, friends and homes for the purposes of bettering their condition, we therefore associate ourselves together under the name of Ferguson's Ferry Protective Claim Association and adopt the following constitution:

" 'First. To elect once a year a president, vice-president, secretary and six directors.

" 'Second. The president to preside, and the vice-president if the president is absent; six members present to constitute a quorum.

" 'Third. Any person taking a claim for farming purposes shall be entitled to three hundred and twenty acres in one body, provided the same shall be in two adjoining squares, and he shall set stakes or mark trees or build mounds, and within ten days shall file said claim with the association.

" 'Fourth. All persons now or heretofore

taking claims shall within sixty days from this date have the following improvements: one log cabin twelve foot square, chinked and covered with poles and a dirt roof.

" 'Fifth. Nothing herein shall be construed to prevent parties from selling their claims when they have complied with the constitution.

" 'Sixth. Any townsite company that has organized or may hereafter be organized, shall be entitled to all lands it can take for the purpose of townsites, provided they do not infringe on the rights of any claimant. In no case should the land taken exceed 1,280 acres.' "

"Sure sounds good to me," said Ernest. "Right nice writin'."

" 'Seventh. Any difficulty concerning claims shall be referred to the managers.

" 'Eighth. All claims made before this date shall be respected if the owner complies with this constitution.

" 'Ninth.' " Ferguson looked around him. "Section nine provides that the president shall call meetings of the board or of the general association.

" 'Tenth. The board of managers shall make the rules for government of the claim association within the rules laid down by the constitution.

" 'Eleventh. The board of managers shall, in the absence of other organized law, have the power to appoint a sheriff and a jury, and to direct the conduct of a trial for any offense against the peace and dignity of man.' "

"Hooray!" shouted Osterman. "I'm for that."

"Twelfth. All persons whose names are attached hereto are hereby declared to be members of this association, and any person desiring the protection of this association shall sign the same and record his claim, for which he will pay the sum of one dollar.

" 'Thirteenth. This constitution may be revised or amended by a two-thirds vote of the members present at a regular meeting, which shall be held on the first Saturday of each month.

" 'Fourteenth. We recognize the decision of the territorial legislature, and hold that each man is entitled to 320 acres if he can locate it without jumping somebody else's claim.' "

Ferguson looked up. "That's it as far as I got with it. If there are any —"

"I move we adopt it!" said Black Gallagher.

"Second the motion."

Ackerman said, "All in favor, say aye."

There was a thunderous chorus of ayes.

"All opposed, say no."

"I'm not sure," said Grimes, "but I ain't voting against it."

"You better not," said Ackerman. "I declare the constitution adopted unanimously."

Ackerman promptly nominated Ferguson for president, and he was elected unanimously; Job Sye was elected Secretary because he could write; and Roy Ernest was elected vice president.

"Now, then," said Ferguson, "you realize that any claim that has the improvement of a cabin as provided in the law cannot be jumped, but any claim that does not have such improvement is jumpable, and we cannot do anything about it."

The men were boisterous. "Now let's hang Keller," said Osterman.

"We have at least three items of business," said Ferguson. "First, to elect six directors. I suggest that be done by written ballot."

After some delay, six directors were elected: Ackerman, who got the most votes, with Simon Hudson, Black Gallagher, the man named Jones who had come over two nights before, Tom Turner, and Bill Benson who was liked by everybody.

Meantime, Job Sye had been writing out the constitution with a lead pencil, and after the election of directors, forty-six men signed the paper.

"Now," said Ferguson, "about the trespass on my property this afternoon. I have claimed — and I will so record with this association, 320 acres, which has the required improvement and somewhat more. This afternoon the man named Simmons drove two hundred head of hogs onto my south quarter, and claimed it was open for pre-emption because of the federal law. I told him to get them off, and got this."

"Not by one man," said Osterman in an awed voice.

"Four men."

"You know who they were?"

"I know them."

"I move the president appoint a sheriff," said Hans Osterman, "and we bring him in for trial. We can draw six jurymen by lot, and the president can appoint all the men he needs to enforce the sentence."

It carried. Then somebody said, "When do we hang George Keller?"

"I will call a meeting for tomorrow night, at which both these men will be tried."

"How about the fellers that massacred you?"

"It was a personal matter, and I do not think it concerns this association yet. If it does, I will say so. What we have to do right now is keep lawlessness down and stop indiscriminate jumping of claims. Simmons also jumped one of Mr. Benson's quarters a few days ago, and I think we can try him on that charge at the same time."

"That right, Benson?" asked Ackerman.

"It sure is. I pulled up his stakes, but he put some more in, and threatened to shoot me if I moved them."

Ackerman nodded. "I reckon we can kill two birds with one stone, all right."

"What'll we do with Keller until tomorrow night?" asked Ernest.

"Leave him where he is," said Job Sye. "He's safe, in there."

"He might get hungry," said Ackerman.

"He'll get a lot hungrier where he's goin'," said Ernest. "I say let's don't waste food on a

181

man who's goin' to hang anyway."

Ferguson agreed. "I see no reason why we should worry about a couple of meals for a man who worried so little about another human being's right to dignity and pride."

"Move we adjourn," said Art Grimes.

"If there is no more business, I declare the meeting adjourned until tomorrow night at the same time, when the sheriff appointed by this association will bring the two prisoners to the bar of justice."

Ferguson went down to the ferry to get the sorrel. Benson went with him, and made a fire of buffalo chips and put on coffee.

"Hello, Ferguson," said a voice from the darkness, and Walking Bird came to the fire, followed by two other Indians, all dressed in woolen pants and checked shirts, wearing moccasins but no hats.

Ferguson filled a tin cup with coffee and handed it to the Indian, who tried it, drank it, and handed it back. Ferguson refilled it and handed it to the next one, and then the next one. Finally Ferguson said, "What brings you here, my friend?"

"No Horse has told me about Logan's threats," said the Indian, "and I am worried. It is true my people — or some of them — are getting money from the whites. I do not encourage it, Ferguson, but what can they do? The whites are pushing them out across the river, moving in on the land, and my people come over here to land that is supposed to belong to them — but over here they have no land, no tipis, no game to hunt. You can't expect my people to starve."

"By no means."

Benson got up and left the fire. Walking Bird and his men sat down.

"But it is going to make trouble, Ferguson. The whites are talking against us, and one of them may start a fight, and then my warriors will throw caution aside."

"I wouldn't like to see it," said Ferguson.

"Nor I. But it may happen. And if you know any way to hold back your people, it would save trouble."

"I am in sympathy with you, but we do not have the same control over our people as you have over yours."

"The Indian doesn't have a chance," said Walking Bird.

Benson returned with a pan of cornbread, and gravely handed it to Walking Bird, who took a piece and handed the pan to his companions. Ferguson watched them eat it, and knew they were hungry. He said to Benson, "You could take the sorrel and go to Turner's for some buffalo meat."

"Chai!" said one of the Otos. *"Peeaiy!"*

"That's Rain in July." Walking Bird explained. "He says buffalo is good — but we did not come here to beg."

"You didn't beg. You're hungry, and I have food."

Walking Bird shook his head.

"If I were hungry and you had food," said Ferguson, "would you let me go hungry?"

Walking Bird looked stonily at the fire.

"I am sending Benson to the tavern to get what he can. I want you to take it to your people."

"I will pay," said Walking Bird finally.

"You will not pay me anything until you get settled."

"I do not know when that will be."

"I am not worried," said Ferguson. "I will take your word."

Benson galloped off in the darkness.

Ferguson looked across the river. "Do your people know anything about sheep?"

Walking Bird nodded. "Some of my people have had sheep in the past. Some still have them."

Rain in July touched Walking Bird's arm. Walking Bird motioned across the river and said: "*Shongtung, natoo.* Coyotes with long hair."

Rain in July nodded. "*Neesh-noungai?* River?" he asked.

Walking Bird nodded.

"Do you know how to get sheep across a river?" asked Ferguson.

Walking Bird smiled. "Sheep have strong notions about crossing water — but we could help."

"Then get your people here. I will pay them."

"When?"

"Tomorrow morning."

Walking Bird shook his head. "They are scattered all over, and it will take longer than that to find them and to convince them it is not a trap."

"There is no time to be lost. I have three days — but there are twelve thousand sheep."

Walking Bird shook his head. "I don't think I can get them before day after tomorrow."

"Do it no later than that — as soon as you can. Meantime, tell your people not to tell what we plan, for fear the whites will organize to stop them. Meantime, I will keep pretending to try to get the sheep across on the ferry."

Walking Bird looked across the river. "You want to move all those sheep?" he asked.

Ferguson poured a last cup of coffee and drank it himself, careful of his cut lips.

"I have to move them by two days from tomorrow night or I lose the ferry," he said quietly.

Walking Bird looked interested for the first time. "Not on the ferry," he said. "The only way you can move so many is to swim them across — and that will take many hands."

"Your people have many hands."

Walking Bird nodded. "Yes, if you give me time."

Ferguson tried the coffee again. "It is the only possibility," he admitted. "I have known that from the beginning."

"Then why did you gamble the ferry?"

Ferguson shrugged. "He was pushing me too far, and he was pushing the emigrants too — and I thought I could beat him and get rid of him."

"He sounds like a bad man."

Ferguson snorted.

"I hope my people stay away from him."

"I hope so too — but don't count on it."

One of the Indians spoke in Oto, and Ferguson nodded. The Indian got up and left silently.

"He has gone to pass the word about the sheep," said Walking Bird. "How much will you pay?"

"A dollar a day."

"It's not much, but a lot better than going hungry. We will work for that."

Ferguson got up, poured out the grounds in the coffeepot, went down to the river and rinsed it out and then filled it. He came back to the fire and set it in a bed of ashes, and got the coffee grinder and a small sackful of beans, and began to turn the handle. When he had the little drawer full of coffee, he poured it into the coffeepot, wrapped up the beans and put them back.

"I think," Walking Bird said with a smile, "that my squaw makes better coffee than you do, but I have never tasted coffee as good as yours tonight."

Ferguson handed him the small quantity of remaining coffee beans. "Give these to her with my compliments," he said.

"No," said Walking Bird. "We are not looking for charity."

"I will take it out of your wages when you move the sheep."

Walking Bird eyed the bag of coffee beans hungrily. "All right," he said with dignity. "It is an advance against my wages."

They sat without talking for a while. The coffee began to boil, and Ferguson poured another round. Then Benson returned with ten pounds of meat slung in a tow sack. He unwrapped it and cut off two big slices and gave them to the Indians, who ate them greedily.

Ferguson said, "Take the rest to your families. They can pay me after we get the sheep across the river."

Walking Bird arose. "I thank you for your thoughtfulness," he said.

"Do me just one favor," said Ferguson. "If any of your people have to go on a massacre, tell them to put it off until we get the sheep into Nebraska."

Walking Bird thought about it for a moment. "If anything like that happens," he said, "whites will hunt us down like animals." He stepped into the darkness and was gone.

Benson looked after him. "Sure speaks good English," he said.

"He ought to," said Ferguson. "He spent twelve years in a mission school."

CHAPTER XIV

ON THE WAY home, he stopped by the tavern and asked about Sally. She was mixing a batch of light-bread dough, and he was relieved to see that she looked unmarked from what must have been a terrifying experience. She said, "When he raised my dress, I didn't know what to think, but —" She shuddered. "There's something wrong with him. What will I do if he comes back?"

"He won't come back," said Ferguson. "Not tonight, anyway. And not tomorrow night or any night after that unless I miss my guess." She smiled gratefully.

"I wonder if you would put some butter on my face," he said.

She was all concern, wiping her hands on her apron. "It must ache terribly."

"It doesn't bother as long as I am moving around, but it might get troublesome during the night."

She went out to the well to pull up the bucket that had the butter in it, and took out a tablespoonful. She lowered the bucket while he held the lantern with a candle in it. Then they went back inside and she spread the butter over his cut and the bruised face with gentle, strong, and skilful fingers. He thanked her for it, and thought of kissing her, but Tom

Turner looked in about that time to see how it was going, and Ferguson smiled at her. "You have nice hands," he said.

She blushed and went back to her kneading.

"I looked at the prisoner a couple of times already," said Turner on the way out. "You reckon he'll be safe?"

"He sure can't get out without help."

"You know anybody who would help him?"

"For certain things, yes — but I don't think they will want to get mixed up in an affair like this."

"If I thought they might try to rescue him, I'd go out there now and shoot him myself."

Ferguson put an arm around Turner's shoulders. "It would be worse than it is already. This man is in our custody, and it is our duty to bring him to trial — not to kill him."

"He better hang!" said Turner, his under jaw working.

"He will hang, all right, but by a group — not by an individual, and not as an act of vengeance, but to keep him from doing it again and to warn others who might be tempted to some such crime."

Ferguson stepped out into the still, dark night. "So long," he said.

He was up early and went to the ferry. "What's it look like across the river?" he asked Benson.

"Too dark to see, but there ain't no fires over

there yet, so I reckon ev'rybody's still asleep."

"Did they ever bring that second bend of sheep down to the dock?"

"Part-way."

"How about the two boys with the sheep over here?"

"They moved 'em up across the slope yesterday, and I reckon they are waitin' for the rest of 'em."

"I'm going across the river," said Ferguson.

Benson looked troubled. "Mr. Ferguson, it ain't none of my business, but it don't look so good for you to get them twelve thousand sheep across the river, does it?"

"Maybe it isn't as bad as it looks."

"It better not be. If you ain't got somethin' up your sleeve, you're gonna lose the ferry."

Ferguson eased the sorrel into the water, and noted that it seemed to be a little lower than the day before. He came out on the Iowa side, and Teddy Root was up and waiting for him.

"Mr. Ferguson, them fellers come back about midnight, and went up there somewheres." He pointed.

Ferguson said, "Apparently they aren't getting up early. I don't see any fires."

"We sure aren't loadin' any sheep."

"You will be."

He rode up to a cleared space before the sheep; a covered cook-wagon stood blackly silhouetted against the early morning sky, and

Ferguson rode up to it and called out: "Anybody home?"

There was no answer. He picked up a stick from the dead fire and beat against the side of the wagon. "Anybody home?" he asked.

A step sounded behind him, and he turned to face Zachariah Mawson, who carried a rifle.

"Who's wakin' people up this time of night?"

"I am," Ferguson said evenly. "Didn't you expect to see me again?"

Mawson said, "Didn't you get enough? You want me to finish grindin' up your face?"

"Not until you have a couple of your boys to hold me. Or a rifle to even up the odds."

Mawson said, "You're pushin' me too far, Ferguson."

"After yesterday," Ferguson said slowly, "I must confess your threats don't scare me."

Mawson glared at him.

"That's the trouble with a threat," said Ferguson. "As soon as you carry it out, the threat no longer has any value."

"The next time," said Mawson, "I'll let some daylight through you."

Ferguson said, "I haven't the slightest doubt you would do that, whether I should happen to be armed or not, but I must be honest and say that it doesn't scare me very much."

"You ain't got sense enough to be scared."

"When a man has so little confidence in his own power that he has two other men hold the man he is fighting — I wonder what your boys

191

think of their brave pa for that."

"Shut up!"

"He botherin' you, pa?" asked a voice from the darkness, and Abner Mawson came alongside his father.

"I can handle him," Mawson said. "Ferguson, what are you comin' here for in the middle of the night?"

"I have come to find out if you called off the bet."

"You tryin' to welsh out?"

"I'm trying to get you to hold up your end of the bet."

"Meanin'?"

"Meaning that the bet was to move your sheep — not to herd them. You are supposed to deliver them to the dock."

"I figgered you'd give up."

"I don't know why you should think that," Ferguson said. "If you don't get those sheep to the dock, there is no bet at all."

"I heard you say that," said the voice of Charlie Logan.

Ferguson waited until Logan and Yeakel came out of the darkness. "I won't say I counted on finding you here," he said, "but I am not surprised."

"Meaning what?" Yeakel demanded.

"I knew that you and Logan and Mawson were in it together."

"In what?" asked Logan.

"In a partnership to lure the emigrants out

here and fleece them out of everything they have."

"You can't prove it," said Yeakel.

"Wait a minute," said Mawson, and stepped forward. "Ferguson, you're a hard man to deal with. Maybe it would be better to have you on our side."

"It would be better for you," said Ferguson, "but not for me. I want to maintain my self-respect."

"You could charge twice as much for ferry passage as you're gettin' now," said Mawson.

"I'm charging enough to suit me. The settlers and emigrants have got all they can do to keep from losing everything they've got to you two."

"Are you including me?" asked Yeakel.

"You make loans on property without justification, because you get a commission whether the loan is good or bad. You charge exorbitant interest because there is no law against it — and half the people who borrow money through you go broke so you can get your commission. You will see a man lose everything he has so you can make fifty dollars."

"It's hard to prove," said Yeakel.

"Hard — but maybe not impossible." The sky was getting lighter, and Ferguson could see them clearly. "And you, Logan, are behind that fake townsite."

"What fake —"

"The Logan City Townsite Company." Ferguson faced them squarely. "Every man who was in on that deal stands to go to the penitentiary, because there is no Logan City Townsite Company, and it is a violation of territorial law to claim a townsite company that has no charter."

Yeakel did not seem to be moved. "Ferguson," he said slowly, "now that you're throwing accusations around, is your own nose clean?"

Ferguson stared at him. "You'd better have a good reason for saying that."

"You're supposed to operate that ferry under a territorial license."

"Yes."

"But the fact is, Ferguson, that you do not have a territorial license. You are operating that ferry solely by virtue of the fact that you got here first."

Ferguson said tightly, "I applied for a license when I first came here, and it was promised — but it has not come through."

Mawson said, "It looks to me like you don't have no special claim on this crossing, Ferguson."

Ferguson said, "The man who thinks that is making a mistake."

"The ferry belongs to you," Mawson conceded, "far as I know — but you've got no exclusive right to operate a ferry on the river."

"There is no other spot within fifteen miles where a ferry could possibly be operated successfully."

"That makes it simple," said Mawson. "Since this is the only spot, and since this place is up for pre-emption, it looks like you're out, no matter which way you take it."

"It may look that way to you," said Ferguson, "but not to me. I am not going to let anybody pre-empt this crossing."

"You may not have nothin' to say about it."

Ferguson ignored it. "I want to know one thing. We made a bet; are you going to stand by your end of it?"

"Yes."

"Then start getting your sheep down to the dock. I can't move sheep without sheep to move."

"You'll never make it," said Yeakel.

"Get the sheep down to the dock," Ferguson repeated. He went down to see Teddy Root and then to untie the lead goat and get her ready.

They had better luck that time, perhaps because the Mawsons had been away for a while and the sheep had had a chance to settle down. They got the first load on board the ferry in twenty minutes, and Teddy Root was cheerful. "Looks pretty good, Mr. Ferguson."

The fact was that even if they kept going like that for the full three days, they would not move two thirds of them; the real hope was in the Otos, and he was counting on Walking Bird, and hoping the Indians would not get into a general state of war before the time was up. Ferguson said, "Keep that Judas goat working. It will encourage the emigrants."

"Say, I been wonderin' why Mawson made that fool bet, Mr. Ferguson, and it just struck me."

"What's the answer!"

"I bet he's broke; he can't pay the ferriage."

Ferguson thought about it for a moment. "You might be right."

"But a-course you won't lose; you can always hold enough sheep to get your money."

The boat moved out, and Ferguson went with it.

The two Mawson boys were waiting on the Nebraska side, and a small crowd of men watched them unload the sheep. Ackerman joined Ferguson at the coffeepot and said, "We got Simmons."

"Where is he?"

"I tied him up and left him in the empty wagon at my place."

"How about Keller?"

"Still there, I reckon."

"It must be pretty hot in that well; it's dry, you know."

Ackerman chuckled. "Hell of a lot hotter where he's goin' tonight."

CHAPTER XV

THEY HELD THE trial in Ferguson's cabin with Job Sye acting as judge, sitting on a stump before the scarred old library table. "Right fancy furniture," he said. "We got nothin' like that."

"I took it for passage," said Ferguson, "and gave the man three dollars to boot. He didn't have any use for it anyway; he was going to Oregon."

Ackerman came in, pushing Simmons ahead of him. Simmons' hands were tied behind him, and he looked disheveled. "I demand to know why you are treating me like this," he said.

Sye was filling his pipe. "Reckon you're about to find out," he said.

"If it's on account of what happened yesterday — that's a personal matter between Ferguson and me, and you've got no right to interfere."

"I heard it was a personal matter," said Sye, "but three other fellers interfered on your side and you never put up no squawk at all."

Simmons stood against a wall, his hands still tied, and Ackerman sat against the wall between Simmons and the door. The men crowded in until the cabin was fairly well crowded, and Job Sye rapped for order.

"Now, then," said Sye, "this here is called a meetin' of the Ferguson's Ferry Protective

Claim Association for the purpose of —"

"What kind of fake outfit is that?" demanded Simmons.

Job Sye looked at him over his glasses. "The prisoner will keep his trap closed until he is addressed by the court," he said quietly.

Ackerman stood up and moved closer to Simmons.

"This ain't no court," said Simmons, "and I ain't —"

Job Sye interrupted. "It looks as if the arrestin' officer will have to take steps," he said.

"Arrestin' officer, hell! This ain't no court! This ain't even —"

He stopped abruptly, for Ackerman dealt him a hard backhanded blow square on the mouth. Simmons looked dazed for a moment, and then tasted the blood from his cut lips but said nothing.

"We want six jurymen," said Sye, "and I figure the best way to choose 'em is by lot. We'll write every man's name on a piece of paper and put 'em all in a hat. Then we'll let somebody pick out six, and them six will be the jury. Agreed?"

There was a murmur of assent. "If anybody don't agree, let him speak up now or shut up later."

He appointed Simon Hudson to collect the slips of paper, and Black Gallagher to pull them out of Art Grimes' droopy-brimmed hat. Gallagher chose the slips without

198

looking, and laid them on the table in front of Sye.

"The first one," said Sye, writing down a name in his minutes, "is Nosey Porter. The second one is Sandy John Ferguson — but he's out. He can't set on the jury. The second one is Dave Ackerman, but he's out. Gallagher draw me a couple more."

Sye unfolded a piece of paper. "We got Osterman, Smithwick from near Tehama, Ernest, Grimes — you git your own hat back —, and Tim Jones. You six fellers step up here and hold up your right hands. You swear to listen to this testimony and to form an unbiased judgment, and render your verdict accordingly?"

They all said, "We do," and took their places, three on each side of the table where Sye was writing.

Simmons began to look scared.

"Now this here is a trial of this here defendant, name of Simmons, for jumping the claim of Sandy John Ferguson, who admits he has two claims for a total of 320 acres, according to territorial law. Mr. Simmons is alleged to have jumped the south quarter yesterday afternoon, and it is up to this jury to say whether he jumped a claim that belonged to somebody else under the rules of this association, and if he did, to set the penalty." He looked at Simmons. "Does the prisoner wish to make a statement at this time?"

"I protest this travesty of just—"

He stopped again, for again Ackerman's big hand was slammed across his mouth, and Simmons looked first shocked, then indignant, and finally subdued as he pushed a tooth out with his tongue, and it fell to the dirt floor.

Sye wrote in his book and said aloud: "Prisoner protests jurisdiction of the court."

"Your honor," said Tim Jones, "how much jurisdiction has the court got?"

"The court assumes jurisdiction as it sees fit," said Job Sye. "I would say it has any jurisdiction it needs as long as it does not conflict with any other court."

Obviously, Ferguson observed to himself, Job Sye had at one time or another been around a court of law more than just a little.

"The complaining witness is Sandy John Ferguson," Sye went on, writing in his minutes, "and I reckon we better hear from him now."

Ferguson went to the table.

"Your name?" asked Sye.

"John Ferguson."

"Raise your right hand and swear to tell the truth, the whole truth, and nothin' but the truth, so help you God."

"I do."

"Go ahead."

"I pre-empted two quarters under the territorial laws of Nebraska, late last fall when I came here," said Ferguson. "There are no legal descriptions because there has been no survey,

200

but I have a cabin on one, and am building a well, and just across the boundary line, the way I measure it, I have a corral and a shed. There was nobody on that land when I came here, and I claimed it."

"Has anybody disputed your claim?"

"Not until yesterday, when Simmons drove two hundred head of hogs on the south quarter. I went over to see if he knew what he was doing, and he said he was claiming that quarter because I had no right to it under federal law. I told him to get off, but he refused."

"You had a fight?"

"He didn't git his face smashed up diggin' goobers," said Nosey Porter.

Sye looked at Porter over his glasses. "The job of the jury is to give a verdict — not to offer testimony," he said coldly.

"Yes, your honor," said Porter.

"Does the witness want to tell about the fight?" Sye asked.

"No, your honor, I do not," said Ferguson.

"Very well. Anything else you want to add?"

"I guess that's all there is."

"Was Mr. Simmons here when you came here?"

"No, he came over about three months ago."

"Has he pre-empted any land around here?"

"Not as far as I know."

"Did he ever tell you he intended to jump your claim?"

"No."

"That's all," said Sye. "Will the defendant take the stand?"

Simmons was sworn in. He looked worried but not alarmed. He said, "I want to ask first, Your Honor, how much authority this jury has."

Sye raised his eyebrows. "All it needs, I guess."

"You mean it can find me guilty?"

"It sure can — and it can fix the punishment."

"How much punishment can it decide?"

"All it wants to, Mr. Simmons."

Simmons licked his lips. "You mean — corporal punishment?"

"Corporal punishment, sure. What's the difference between corporal punishment or any other kind?"

"Well, I — what kinds of corporal punishment?"

Sye puffed on his pipe. "It could have a man whipped if it wanted to."

"Whipped?" Simmons was pretty well beaten down by now.

"Yup — or hanged, if it takes a notion."

Simmons turned pale. "This jury could sentence me to be hung?"

"The jury wouldn't sentence you, Mr. Simmons. The court sentences — but the jury can fix the punishment. Now do you want to talk about the charge agin' you?"

"That land was laying there, doing nothin',"

said Simmons, "and I needed some land for my hogs, so I took it. Then John Ferguson came along and ordered me off, and naturally I fought back. That's a man's right, ain't it?"

Sye thought it over. "I reckon it would depend on what he was fightin' for, and how he fought back."

"I have got some things to say," said Ferguson.

"All right, fire away."

"This land was in use. I pastured two or three mules and two oxen on it all the time. Besides that, there is a corn crop that takes about fifty feet down one side."

"You got a fence on it?"

"I haven't seen a quarter-section fence this side of Iowa, but I fenced my corn to keep the stock out."

"I just thought I'd ask," Sye explained.

"Do I have the court's permission to ask the defendant a question?"

Ferguson faced Simmons. "Who sent you to jump my claim?" he asked.

"Nobody sent me."

Ferguson smiled. "Then you admit that you jumped it?"

"I don't admit nothin'," Simmons said hastily, "it was open land and I took it."

"Why did you take it?"

"Because —" He hesitated. "Because I needed some land. That's reason enough, ain't it?"

"Not if the land belongs to somebody else. And certainly not when you have already jumped a quarter that had been pre-empted by Mr. Benson."

Simmons hesitated, then decided to brazen it out. "He wasn't usin' his."

"You did claim it, then?"

"I put stakes on it."

"Are you a farmer by occupation?"

"I been mostly farmin' all my life."

"A hog farmer?"

"Not exactly," said Simmons, "but I know about hogs."

"Did you bring this drove of hogs with you when you came to Nebraska territory?"

"Well, of course not. Everybody knows that."

"Then, Mr. Simmons, how long *have* you had them?"

"I —" He saw the trap, but he did not see a way out. "Not very long."

"Three days?"

"No-o."

"Two days?"

"Two days today."

Ferguson persisted. "Then you bought these hogs yesterday morning?"

Simmon's eyes were desperate as he saw the trap close in.

"You have a bill of sale?"

"I never thought to ask for one."

"Pretty careless, wasn't it, to buy two hundred head of hogs without a bill of sale?"

"I knew who I was buying from."

"What was the price?"

Simmons looked at Sye. "I don't have to answer that, do I?"

Sye scratched his head. "I don't reckon it is material, Mr. Ferguson."

"Perhaps not — but this one is: from whom did you buy those hogs, Mr. Simmons?"

Simmon's mouth opened. "I — —" He looked at Sye. "Do I have to answer that?"

"Your Honor," said Ferguson, "if necessary, I will tell this court about the three men who joined Mr. Simmons to give me this face, and I want to know if he bought these hogs from one of those men. Also, I want to know if he bought them at all. I believe he is only a hired hand for somebody else. I don't think he ever owned those hogs, but that the legal owner hired him to drive them onto my land to harass me."

Sye puffed at his pipe. "Sounds like a legitimate question," he said to Simmons.

"Now tell us," said Ferguson, "did you actually own those hogs?"

Simmons debated it in his mind, and it became obvious that he decided to lie. "Yes, I owned them."

"Then where did you buy them?"

"That's a business secret."

"Two hundred hogs ain't no business secret," said Sye, and wrinkled his nose. "I can smell 'em from here."

"I can't tell," Simmons said nervously.

"Your Honor," said Ferguson, "maybe he's *afraid* to tell. Then I would like to suggest to this court that the legal owner of the hogs, was and still is a man named Zachariah Mawson, who is across the river with twelve thousand head of sheep, and who wants to get rid of me so he can have the ferry and control the entire area."

There was dead silence in the cabin, and finally Sye said: "I suppose you know what you're talkin' about."

"It is not an idle accusation, Your Honor." He turned to Simmons. "Now, then, you went through all this to give Mawson an excuse to bring his ruffian sons across the river and give me a whipping, didn't you?"

Simmons' face was white. "No, sir, that wasn't it."

"You still say you own the hogs?" asked Sye. "Yes."

"But no bill of sale."

"I didn't get one."

"Well," said Sye. "It sure don't sound like you own no hogs as far as I can figure it."

Porter spoke up. "Your Honor, can the jury ask the witness a question?"

"Yes."

"Was it a surprise to you, Mr. Simmons, when Mawson and his two boys came out to help you?"

"Well, yes."

"You mean you didn't know they was in the neighborhood?"

"No."

"Then how come I seen you with 'em at Chippewa City a couple of hours earlier?"

Simmons bit his lip, a badly harassed man. "All right," he said, "I did know it."

"Then the hogs wasn't yours at all. They belonged to Mawson."

"They was mine," Simmons insisted.

Ferguson was puzzled. Then a light dawned. "May I suggest that he was promised the hogs if he would jump my claim?"

Sye raised his eyebrows. "Sounds likely."

"They were my hogs," Simmons insisted.

"But no bill of sale," said Sye.

"I can get one."

"Not in time for this trial," said Sye, "because it's over." He turned to the jury. "You fellers go outside and elect a foreman, and make your decision. And don't be too long, because them hogs stink like hell."

The six men got up and went out. The men in the room began to talk. Ferguson looked for butter to put on his face, but settled for lard.

Within a few minutes the jury was back, and Nosey Porter stood up. "I was elected foreman," he said, "and we come to the following conclusions regarding the case: First, that Sandy John Ferguson had a pre-emption claim on the quarter; second, that Simmons jumped it knowingly and with felonious intentions."

"Felonious intentions?" asked Sye.

"Yes, Your Honor. One of the men on the jury thought that ought to go in somewhere."

"Go ahead," said Sye.

"We recommend the following: First, that Simmons be required to pay Ferguson five cents a day per hog for use of his pasture; second, that Simmons be required to get out there with a shovel and a wagon and clean up all the mess left by them hogs; third, that them two hundred head of hogs don't belong to nobody, and that the Ferguson's Ferry Protective Claim Association take charge of them, to be cared for or disposed of in whatever way seems fittin', and the proceeds to be saved for a reasonable time and then applied to anything the club votes; fourth, in case they do turn out to belong to somebody, that feller be fined $500 for usin' said hogs to perform a malicious trespass." He looked sternly at Simmons. "And fifth, that Simmons be taken down to the river and held under water for one minute unless he signs a quitclaim deed to Ferguson's south quarter; if he refuses to sign, he will be held under water for a minute and ten seconds, and if he still refuses, for a minute and twenty seconds, and so on until he signs the quitclaim."

"That's murder!" shouted Simmons.

"Sixth," Porter went on. "The defendant admitted he jumped Mr. Benson's claim, and this jury recommends that as soon as he signs a quitclaim for Ferguson's quarter, they take him

208

back to the river and persuade him to sign a quitclaim of Benson's quarter."

Job Sye laid down his pipe. "I have got here a couple of quitclaim deeds, which you can sign now and save yourself a wet night."

"You mean you're goin' to do that tonight?" asked Simmons desperately.

"No use waitin', far as I see. You can wait here while we try the next prisoner."

"Who?"

"George Keller, for attempted rape and unnatural practices."

Simmons asked, "What are you goin' to do to him?"

Sye raised his eyebrows. "Hangin's really too good for him, but we may have to be satisfied with it."

"Hangin'?"

Sye looked at the man's ashen face and protruding eyes. "Sure, you know — rope around his neck." He leaned his head to the left and made the sign of a knife. "Sheriff, you go get the prisoner. Maybe you better take a couple of husky fellers with you to pull him out of that well."

"I'll take Osterman and Porter."

"You fellers git a move on. We got a lot of work to do tonight after the trial."

"We'll hurry," said Ackerman.

"Court's recessed until they git back," said Sye, and all went outside to breathe the night air and to light up their smokes or bite off fresh chews of plug. The air wasn't clean any more, for the south breeze brought the smell of hogs over them like a blanket.

"Sure was a dirty trick," said Simon Hudson. "No question about it."

While he waited, Ferguson went over to the well and saw that the bucket had brought up a new kind of sand. He felt it, and it seemed to be wet. He had better go down into the well in the morning and see what it looked like.

He heard the committee galloping back, and Ackerman rode into the yard and pulled up with a flourish. "He's gone!" he said. "Plumb gone! No hide nor hair! He was down there at sunset, but he ain't there now!"

CHAPTER XVI

WHEN THE EXCITEMENT was over, Ackerman and some twelve or fourteen men took Simmons down to the river, while Ferguson went to the tavern for something to eat.

Sally waited on him, and while she set the table, she said: "Mr. Ferguson, the Otos are on the rampage, they say up at the Forks."

"That's talk," Ferguson said easily.

Her blue eyes were wide. "No, sir, I don't think it is, because on the way home I rode through a whole band of Indians going toward the Forks. They stopped me and talked ugly, but Walking Bird came up and told them to leave me alone."

"Thank goodness."

"Walking Bird said I should tell you that some of his men have been treated badly by some of the whites, and are getting hard to hold back."

"Then there's nothing for it but to be ready to defend ourselves."

"Walking Bird said to tell you he is persuading some of his men to work for you."

"Good," said Ferguson. "Now, Sally —" He took her by the shoulders. "Listen carefully to this."

Her blue eyes were big as they watched his.

"If Indians come into the tavern, either front

or back, don't talk to them, don't say a word. Just very quietly and casually walk away, get out of sight, and stay out of sight."

"They might be hungry."

"They might also be inflamed by war talk; might come here with honest intentions, but they might change their minds when they see you. Do you understand?"

"I think so."

He stood up and looked down at her soberly.

"This is a deadly serious proposition," said Ferguson. "A peaceful-looking Indian can turn into a maniac in an instant — and then it will be too late. Don't take any chances."

She studied him. "Why are you so fussed over me, Mr. Ferguson? Why not — why not Mrs. Talbot?"

"I —" He looked into those large blue eyes, and breathed the faint, clean aroma of her hair. "Well," he said, "I feel different about you, Sally. I —" He took her into his arms, and she came willingly. "Sally, I love you," he said. Isn't that enough reason?"

She stood on her bare tiptoes and threw her arms around him and kissed him on the lips. "It sure is," she whispered.

Obie came into the kitchen with a load of wood, and she backed away and ran to the kitchen.

Noah came in behind Obie, put down his wood, and entered the dining room. "There's sign of water in the well," he said, "and I thought maybe you better take a look, Mr. Ferguson, before it's too late."

"I noticed the sand was damp. Tell you what: you go down to the ferry and help Mr. Benson for a few hours while I have a look at the well. I can let myself down, and Obie can come over in a couple of hours and get me out."

Sally looked in. "I'll come over and pull you up," she said.

He looked at her radiant face, and his pulse quickened and he felt as if she were the only girl on earth — and she was his. "Good," he said, trying to sound businesslike. "Let Sally come over. The mule is prob'ly running from the hogs, but he won't go far from that corn." He smiled. "He's waitin' for it to tassel."

"I'll see that you get out, Mr. Ferguson," she said.

Obie asked, "What can I do?"

"You can come with Sally, in case she needs help. Until this Indian trouble settles down, you'd better not ride around the country alone." And he thought, but did not say, that George Keller was somewhere loose in the countryside, and it could well be that in his twisted mind he would see Sally as the cause of his trouble, and would consider it his right to take whatever perverted vengeance he could imagine.

Sally started back to the kitchen, but pounding hooves sounded outside. The horse stopped suddenly, and a man flung himself from the saddle and ran heavily into the tavern; it was Black Gallagher. "Mr. Ferguson," he shouted, "we wuz down along the river, huntin' Keller, and lookin' around the dock — and we found Bill Benson with his throat cut."

Ferguson was stunned. "Dead?" he asked senselessly.

Gallagher nodded.

"Mr. Benson? I can't — you sure?"

Gallagher nodded.

Ferguson started for the door. "Who did it?" he asked.

"Nobody knows."

Ferguson galloped down to the ferry. They had laid Benson's body on the dock, but there was no blanket over it, and a swarm of flies buzzed around it. Ferguson walked near, took off his hat, and looked down for a moment, hardly seeing the ugly, half-severed neck. Finally he turned away and said, "Better bury him this afternoon. Mr. Porter, I heard you can build a coffin."

"Yes, sir."

"Then build a good one for Mr. Benson. I will pay for it. Noah."

"Yes, sir."

"You stay here and take care of the ferry on this side."

"Yes, sir."

"Mr. Porter, what do you make of this?"

"Either Injuns or George Keller."

"Where did you find him?"

Porter led him to a spot just under the dock, where it was damp but not under water. "Layin' right there."

"No signs of blood," said Ferguson.

"Nope."

"That means they hauled the body here from where he was killed — but why?"

Porter shook his head.

"It sure wouldn't be Injuns," said Art Grimes.

"No," said Ferguson. "It seems to me that he must have been killed to keep him from talking."

"Keller would not have done it, because it don't make any difference to Keller who sees him. We all know he escaped."

"But somebody had to help him escape."

"Must be Mawson," said Roy Ernest. "He seems to be runnin' things over here."

"Or more likely Logan or Yeakel," said Ferguson. "Mawson would more likely do it openly. Logan or Yeakel would not want to be caught. So Benson must have come upon them as they were pulling Keller out of the well, and Keller killed him so he couldn't tell. Did anybody examine the footprints around the well?"

"I looked 'em over," said Art Grimes, "but they was too many. About all I could be sure of was that one set had small feet. It was too dusty to hold much sign," he said.

"That wouldn't be Mawson," said Ferguson.

"Major Yeakel has small feet," said Ernest. "Maybe we'd better talk to him."

"We'll give him a trial!" said Gallagher.

"No. Let's don't get so we try everybody for everything. We don't have any real evidence at all except that Yeakel has small feet — and hundreds of people have small feet."

"Dave Ackerman's party is comin' up from the river," said Porter. "Wonder if they had any luck."

"Hard to say. Is that Simmons with them?"

"Yeah, riddin' in the saddle with his head down and floppin'. Wonder if they drownded him."

"I want somebody to go with me to Benson's cabin," said Ferguson. "Ernest, you want to go?"

"I'll go — but I got to get home first and get my old woman some wood to make dinner."

"I'll meet you here right after dinner. Nobody will bother his place until then. Mr. Grimes, gather some men and see if you can find Mr. Benson's murderer — but don't hang anybody. Then we'll have to have trial."

"Yes, sir."

Roy Ernest rode off, his long legs jogging awkwardly.

Ackerman came up with a paper in his hand. "He was pretty stubborn," he said, "but we was stubborner."

Ferguson looked at Simmons, who had not raised his head. "You didn't go too far, did you?"

"We might' near *had* to," said Ackerman. "But I reckon he's still alive."

"How long did he hold out?" asked Porter.

"We was up to two minutes and ten seconds, and I thought he would bust."

"And your watch don't run very good," said Osterman.

Ferguson folded the papers and put them inside his shirt. He looked at Simmons again. "You sure he's alive?"

"He may be full of water," said Ackerman, "but he was alive when we drug him out, because he signed the quitclaims."

Ferguson said sharply, "Look up, Simmons!"

To his relief, the man slowly raised his head — but Ferguson was shocked, for Simmons had aged twenty years during the night. His face was gray and drawn, his eyes were haunted and lifeless.

"If you want any claim at all on those hogs, you get them off my place and clean up that hundred and sixty acres," said Ferguson. "If you want to tell who hired you to jump my claim, I'll help you clean up the land."

Simmons looked dully at him but said nothing.

"You might as well turn him loose," said Ferguson.

"Suits me," said Ackerman. "Now we can all go after Keller."

"One thing, Mr. Ackerman: Mr. Benson has been murdered, but you must not hang anybody or take any other summary action. The guilty man must be brought to trial in legal fashion before we undertake any punishment — and any man who unnecessarily kills such a man will be guilty of murder himself."

Ackerman grinned. "You'd have a hell of a hard time getting a jury to convict anybody for killing George Keller."

Ferguson went on. "Another thing: we want him alive long enough to ask him questions. Keller is working for somebody, and it would help it we could get him to say who that person is."

"If he swallers enough river water, he will talk," said Tim Jones.

"Not if he has a bullet-hole between the eyes," said Ferguson, looking hard at Ackerman.

Ackerman grinned. "All right, I will try to get him here alive."

"If you see a bunch of Otos headed this way, don't start shooting until you find out what they're up to."

"With Injuns," said Roy Ernest, "you got to act first or it's too late."

"Give them a chance," said Ferguson. "I have asked Walking Bird to get a crew together to help me with the sheep."

"We'll remember that," said Black Gallagher, "but if one of them red-skinned critters comes wavin' a bloody scalp, I'll shoot first."

Ferguson looked at Obie, who had been listening with bulging eyes. "Obie, you go back to the tavern with me. I've got to take a look at that well and see what's going on down there. It might be that it needs just a little more digging to be a well."

Ackerman rode a little way with him. "Mr. Ferguson, we're worried on account of that bet you made with Mawson. We could all pitch in and help, and we might git them woollies acrost the river in time."

Ferguson said, "I'm figuring on the Indians' helping me do it."

"Swimmin'?" Ackerman asked dubiously.

"You shoulda stopped the bet when Mawson didn't bring his sheep to the dock," said Porter.

"No," said Ferguson. "This man is going to harass us one way or another, and he is especially going to harass me because he wants the ferry. I would rather stick to this, because I still expect to win, and then we won't have so much trouble with him. Maybe he will even leave the country."

"We can help."

"You keep hunting Keller. He's loose and he's dangerous. Anyway, moving sheep is not a job for just anybody. I will need a crew of sheepmen to handle twelve thousand sheep, and I am gambling on the Indians."

"When do you expect to start?" asked Porter.

"Right after dinner I will take a small band across, and find out if the lead goat will do her job swimming. I might find a couple then that will help to lead the rest of them. I'm not worried — unless something unforeseen happens."

Porter rode off with Benson's body across the saddle of a mule that had wandered in — probably the mule which Benson had ridden to the ferry. Ferguson and Obie rode back to the tavern, and Ferguson told Sally: "You can come to pull me out in about two hours. And bring Obie with you."

She smiled softly to suggest the secret between them, and he smiled in return.

"Mind what I say," he insisted. "Don't come alone."

"I will mind," said Sally. "If you order me, I will mind!"

CHAPTER XVII

HE WENT BACK to his own cabin and got a pair of horsehide gloves. He lifted the bucket into the well, took a firm hold on the rope, and stepped into the bucket and began to pay out the rope around the handle of the bucket.

In a moment he was down fifty feet, and the hole above looked small against the cloudless, light blue sky.

At a hundred feet he doubled the rope and took two turns around the handle of the iron bucket, and stopped for a few minutes. At a hundred and fifty feet he stopped again.

Then he drew a deep breath and began to loosen the rope. He dropped more slowly to the two-hundred-foot level, and stopped to let his eyes adjust themselves before going on to the bottom.

He went on slowly, hoping to hear the slap of water against the bottom of the bucket. When he finally did hear it, the bucket immediately came to bottom on the sand. Keeping a hold on the rope and one hand on the bucket, he stepped out.

He got back in the bucket and pulled himself up, hand over hand.

He got the tools and went back down, tied the rope and stepped out. He set the bucket to one side and began to probe with the shovel.

He dug in a couple of feet on one side, went through a hard layer of clay, and was gratified to observe that water accumulated there pretty rapidly. He watched the water oozing out of the face of the sand, and realized that there was already enough to make a steady stream as big as his little finger.

He had been down about two hours, he figured, and it was time for Sally and Obie to come after him. He poked around a little more, and watched the water level begin to rise. He loaded the tools in the bucket and was prepared for Sally's voice to come from far above. But after a while the water was six inches deep, and still she had not called.

When he looked up again, the sun was gone, and he guessed it was one o'clock, and began to worry. He wondered if Sally and Obie could have fun afoul of the Otos.

The water was a foot deep, and rising at the rate of fifty gallons an hour; the flow had increased steadily.

By three o'clock, however, with the water steadily rising, and now up to his knees, he began to consider trying to hoist himself; perhaps he could make it in relays.

At four o'clock he estimated that the water would be six feet deep in twelve more hours, and he would then have to stand on the bucket. By that time he faced the fact that apparently nobody was coming after him, and he would have to get out by himself. He would have to try the rope.

He figured to pull on the rope, and that would take his weight off the bucket; he would go hand over hand as far as he could in safety, and then perhaps coil the rope around his body until his hands regained their strength.

He stepped into the bucket, took up the slack of the rope, and began to pull, hand over hand. As he pulled his weight off the bucket, the bucket rose as far as it could; then he transferred his hold and pulled again. He got up about ten feet, but the bucket caught its rim in an unusually wide crack between two planks. He jerked hard — and, without warning, the bucket fell away from under him and he went down with it.

The water cushioned the drop, but he struck the backs of his thighs against the rim of the iron bucket, and for an instant could not straighten up. Then he became aware of two hundred feet of rope falling on top of him; he leaped out of the bucket and straightened up against the side of the well as flat as possible, and watched unbelievingly as the rope dropped into the well. It filled the bottom incredibly fast, and he finally realized that actually there were two ropes falling.

The ropes filled the well, loosely stacked, to about his shoulders, and in the passage of a breath it was all over.

He climbed on top of the pile of rope, and it occurred to him to wonder why the rope had broken. He found the two ends and stared at them in the dimness; he felt them both with his fingers, and there was no doubt of it: the rope had been cut. Not cut entirely in two, but almost in two, so that he might very well have dropped the full distance. It was a miracle that he had not — the miracle of the bucket rim's catching the crack.

He looked up at that tiny hole in the sky, and now it looked miles away. He tried to holler, but after a while he was hoarse.

He had tools, and he thought of digging out at a slant, but he knew the dangers of shifting earth when a man was digging from underneath, and he also realized that it might take weeks.

He looked up at that sky again. It was now so far away. For a few feet he could see the serrated line of the planking; then it was lost in the gloom, and he realized the sun was getting low. He had been in the well all day, and he noticed that the water now was about up to the top of the pile of rope.

He looked up again. The sky was a very dark blue, and he supposed the sun had gone down. He knew now that there was no hope of rescue that night.

He sat on top of the coil of rope until about ten o'clock, when the sky lightened a little, and he knew the moon was up. He could not see much except stars, and presently, against the deep purple of the sky, the serrated column of planks on one side of the well.

Wait a minute! Those serrated edges! The sections of planking all sloped in at the top, out at the bottom. They would provide good hand-holds and fair footing. Was it possible he could *climb* his way out of the well?

He stood up, calculating. He could lift himself from one edge to the next. He would have to test every section to be sure it was solid, for it was too dark to see.

He pulled himself up until he stood on the bottom section with his hands on top of it. Then he moved his hands to the top of the next section above, and brought his feet up to the next ledge.

He did not look down, but he counted the sections. There were approximately eighty sections, and that meant eighty lifts. He went up ten sections, and had seventy to go, and already his toes ached from the strain. Thirty feet up; he had over two hundred feet to go.

He went up another ten sections, and his strength began to give. He went up a third set of ten, and his upper arms ached painfully. He went up a fourth set of ten, and was halfway, but his fingers were almost totally numb, his feet were like lumps, and his upper arms were lanced through and through with sharp, stabbing pains. He would have given ten years of his life for a rest.

He tried to brace himself with his legs across to the opposite side, but the distance was too far. He started up again, and this time tried to transfer the lift to his thighs. It worked fine for the fifth set of ten, but then suddenly his thighs went weak, and he was faced with the fact that soon it would be an impossibility to raise himself with his legs. He had felt them almost give way on the last two sections, so he switched to his arms, and at the first pull he felt the sharp pain cut through the backs of his upper arms, and now the muscles in his forearms seemed to feel it.

He saw the moon go straight over, and knew he had been there longer than he thought. It must be around one o'clock. Three hours on that wall and he had gone fifty sections! Now the only problem was how to go the last thirty sections — the last ninety feet.

He caught his fingers sliding off the edge of a plank, and switched for a while to the sides of his palms. He pulled up three times with his arms, and then once with his legs. He alternated from a straight side pull to a corner pull; he changed from fingers to the edges of his palms, hanging on grimly, desperately; he watched his feet, turned them as flat as he could so he could step on the whole length of them, and found some relief.

He made it up the sixth set of ten. Two more sets to go. He kept moving, and now became super-cautious, for he was near to freedom, and he did not want to waste the painful effort he had put in already.

He tested every section to be sure there were no loose boards, he went up one section and then moved around slowly, changing his weight as well as he could from one set of muscles to another. In that fashion he made it to the top of the seventh set of ten sections. The eighth and ninth sets left him exhausted.

He started up the last set of ten and moved to the corner, careful that his feet should not misstep. He went up two sections that way, carefully feeling his way along the top of each plank with his almost senseless fingers, then clinging with the side of his palm or the heel of the palm or even the heel of the thumb. His hands were raw and bleeding and the slipperiness of his own blood was a hazard.

Slowly, laboriously he made his way up the third section. The pains now shot through his entire back, through his hips, through the calves of his legs, through his thighs when he used them. His neck ached from looking up, and he quit doing that because he could see nothing but stars anyway. He got up five sections and rested for a moment, his face flat against the rough wood.

He willed himself up another section and then another.

Three sections to go. Only three sections. He rested a little, moved to the corner, kept lifting his hands and putting them down, beating the backs of his fingers to restore circulation, drawing them hard across the rough wood.

He went up another, and for a moment felt a lift as he calculated how close he was to delivery. Then he felt for the next one, and his first hand slipped off. He shook his fingers loosely, and then tried again. He found the edge and clung to it, went up one more.

One more to go. One more section. He was elated, but he must be careful. No slips now. He went up — and bumped his head squarely on top.

For a moment he saw stars, but he held on, wondering. Then he knew something he had completely forgotten: the curbing at the top of the well was built out over the well itself. The well was four feet wide and the curbing had a three-foot opening. The curbing was of bricks and something like two feet high. He tried to reach the top of the curbing from where he was, but the offset prevented him. To be stopped now, two and a half feet from solid earth. There had to be a way out.

He looked for a possible rope hanging from the pulley, but of course there was none. He looked at the pulley itself, and a thought struck him. It was mounted on an iron shaft laid across the walls of the curbing, and he would not have to reach around an offset to get to it. He could see its outline plainly against the stars, and reached for it, but missed it by three inches.

He studied it for a moment, and finally worked his way to the other side of the well, trying each side as he went, to see if he could reach. But he could not. With his passion for symmetry and orderliness, he had put the pulley in the exact center of the well, and it was three inches from his fingers at any point.

He knew that he could not hang there very long. The effort of reaching had weakened him already. He looked again at the pulley, outlined against the stars, and realized there was now only one choice: he had to jump for the pulley.

He made sure he was in the right place; he tested the footing; he leaned far out, holding with one hand, reaching with the other. He felt the one hand slip for the last time, with no other hand to relieve it, and no time to get it down. He went through a fleeting instant of blinding panic, and then he leaped with all the power he could summon from his flagging muscles. He felt his fingers close around the rim of the pulley, and he swung free in the well. His other hand found the pulley, and with one last impossible effort he swung his legs up and through the opening until he lay on his back on the curbing. He got one hand on the curbing and pulled himself clear, and fell on the ground outside.

He lost consciousness for a while out of sheer exhaustion and long-anticipated relief, and then the cool morning air revived him. Presently he got to his knees and then to his feet and went into his cabin. He lay at full length on the floor for a while, and felt some strength flow into his arms and legs and back and shoulders. Finally he got up. The sorrel was nowhere around, and he set off down the road on foot for Turner's Tavern.

CHAPTER XVIII

FOR A WHILE he lurched through the dust, following the trail unconsciously, but after a time the early-morning crowing of Nosey Porter's much-prized Plymouth Rock rooster came to him from across the prairie. With relief he began to realize that he was out of the well, and alive, and for the first time he could take a deep, free breath, and feel grateful that he was walking on the road instead of lying in a pulpy mass at the bottom of the well.

He shuddered in the early-morning air, and the long nightmare of terror and strain came over him anew, and he broke out in a cold sweat as he remembered the three inches that had stood between him and death.

But he kept moving forward, and was relieved when at last he saw the Turner road-ranch, because, for a while he had wondered if the Otos had actually rampaged through the country. But now the light smoke ascending straight into the still morning air and the fragrant smell of burning cedar assured him that the Indians were still under control.

He was within a quarter of a mile of Turner's when a man galloped up from the river on a black horse, jumped off in front of Turner's, and ran inside without tying the horse.

Ferguson tried to run, but fell down; he was

so drugged with fatigue that he did not at once get up. Then finally he got to his feet, shook his head and went the rest of the way. He ducked under the low door-frame and heard Logan's voice: "I'll find him. That much I promise you."

Tom Turner, looking up in astonishment as Ferguson entered, said soothingly, "I don't think he never done nothin', Mr. Logan."

Ferguson looked at the man's triangular face and very black beard, and remembered what No Horse had told him about Logan. "What about No Horse?" he asked.

Logan stared at him. "He cut Benson's throat, and I'm going to find him." He moistened his lips; then he said: "You're defending him."

"I don't need to defend him. He hasn't done anything."

Logan's eyes were fiery. "He'll hang for this. I'll see he does!"

Ferguson said with scorn, "Quit trying to buy an Indian squaw, and No Horse won't have to chase you off the reservation."

Logan rushed at him, hit him once, and Ferguson went down. Logan started to kick him in the throat, but Tom Turner's voice stopped him: "Hold it, Logan!"

The editor recovered his balance and turned to look into the twin barrels of the shotgun.

Turner said, "You come from the river. Maybe you just left the reservation, like Ferguson said."

Ferguson got up slowly. "Maybe he got kicked out of the village again."

"I'm warning you," said Logan, "that Injun is no good. I'll get him and he'll hang."

Ferguson watched him go.

Turner said, "Where you been? I didn't see you all day yesterday."

Ferguson looked at him and started to answer, then changed his mind about what he would say. "I've been up at my place," he said.

"Grimes and Ackerman was both by, and they couldn't raise you."

Ferguson saw, from the corner of his eye, that Sally was looking in from the kitchen. He knew already that nothing untoward had happened, but now he was puzzled and hurt that they took his disappearance so casually. So he said, "I wasn't too far away." At the same time he wanted to ask Sally what had happened to her, but wouldn't say anything until she came in.

Tom brought him some water. "You hungry?" he asked.

"Tol'able," said Ferguson. "How about pancakes?"

"Sure."

Ferguson heard Sally whip the batter a couple of times with the big iron spoon, then heard the batter sizzle as she poured it into a frying pan.

"Anything happen yesterday?" asked Ferguson.

Turner looked at him quizzically. "Well, not much more than I said. Roy Ernest was by, lookin' for you to go to Mr. Benson's cabin with him; said he'd wait."

"Has anybody made plans for the funeral?"

"They held it up, waitin' for you — but Job Sye went acrost and got Reverend Sledge to preach over him this afternoon."

"What about the ferry?"

"Obie went down to help Noah on this end, and they brought fourteen loads of sheep acrost yesterday. Pretty good day's work, sounds like to me."

"That's around twenty-four hundred head."

"Twenty-five hundred and twenty," Turner said proudly.

"Where are the boys this morning?"

"They was up early," Turner chuckled. "I reckon they figured to move more today than yesterday."

"What about Mawson?"

"He was around, but he and his men didn't help. It was the emigrants that helped Teddy Root."

Sally came in with the pancakes, set them down in front of Ferguson without looking at him, and went back. He watched her go, wondering what had happened: he noted that she apparently had something on beneath her dress, and guessed that she had spent the night fashioning a petticoat out of flour-sacks. She was a good girl and would make a good wife.

Suddenly he wanted to jump up and grab her and ask what was the matter, but he thought better of it, for she might have changed her mind about him. A few hour's delay wouldn't hurt, he thought, and it might bring an easier answer.

Ferguson looked around for coffee but saw none. Turner noticed the movement and said quickly, "I'll get it for you."

Ferguson stared at him as he waddled to the kitchen.

Something was bothering Tom too, and when he returned, Ferguson looked at him and was about to ask him what it was, when Tom turned away — hurriedly, it seemed to Ferguson — and took his place by the beer keg.

Ferguson drank the coffee gratefully, and when it was empty and Tom had returned, he asked: "Where is Mr. Benson's body?"

"They took it to Roy Ernest's. He had the young'uns sleep in the wagon."

"Is there any evidence as to who did it?"

"I reckon not," said Turner.

"You hear what happened to Simmons?"

"He took out — was up to the Forks, last I heard, tryin' to tie onto a wagon train." Turner looked suddenly at Ferguson. "D'ye suppose he had anything to do with the murder?"

Ferguson frowned. "I can't see any good reason why he should have killed Mr. Benson. That would not have restored the land to him."

Ferguson put down his fork and got up. "No matter what happens," he said, "I am going to find the man who killed Mr. Benson."

Turner eyed him obliquely. "You better take care of them sheep first."

"I'm going to." He looked at the door. "Who's coming now?"

"It's a woman," said Turner. "She come from Mrs. Talbot's direction — but it ain't Mrs. Talbot."

Ferguson began to feel some strength in his legs again. They were sore, but they had muscle.

The door opened and a woman stepped in. She was very similar to Mrs. Talbot, but smaller and rather profusely wrinkled, though she did not seem old.

She looked at Tom Turner. "Is this Turner's road-ranch?" she demanded.

"Yes, ma'am."

"I came to find out —" She espied Ferguson, and advanced to where she could snap her fingers under his nose. "What have you done with them?" she demanded.

"Who is 'them'?" asked Ferguson.

"First, you killed her husband. Then you committed mayhem on *my* husband, and he has not been back since."

"I have seen him," said Ferguson. "Maybe he didn't want to go back."

"And now you've done away with her."

Ferguson squinted. "Who's her?"

"My sister, Mrs. Talbot."

"I haven't done anything with her," said Ferguson. "Have you been to her cabin?"

"I have," she said righteously, "but she isn't there."

Turner said, "Mrs. Talbot is of age, and it ain't our job to keep track of her."

"She's my sister — my own sister, and you broke her husband's back."

"It was a fair fight," he said, "and the back-breaking was an accident." He watched the woman wring her hands, and knew she was wrought up, and could well understand why. He said gently, "Mrs. Wiggins, we'll try to find your sister; I don't think she's very far away. And your husband probably will appear around the ferry sometime today."

"I've got to have him," she said brokenly, and tears began to drop down her cheeks. "I can't take care of the oxen, and I have no money for food. I —" She began to cry aloud.

Ferguson gave her a gold piece. "Consider this a loan," he said.

She stared at him through her tears. "From you — the bone-breaker?"

He shrugged. "Usually the worst of men has a good streak in him. It's not a thing I ever count on," he said steadily, "but sometimes it's a pleasant surprise."

She looked at the ten-dollar piece in her hand, and started to give it back to him, but Ferguson said: "It is money honestly made, Mrs. Wiggins, and I hope you will keep it as long as you need it. Children have to eat, and they do not understand a mother's being out of money."

She started to cry again, and Ferguson slipped out. Turner could comfort her; Ferguson had other business at hand. He looked around for a horse or mule to ride to the ferry, but saw nothing but Mrs. Wiggins' horse. He walked toward the well and discovered the sorrel eating corn from a wooden bucket near by. He took the saddle of the well curbing and put it on the sorrel and cinched it up. The sorrel had finished eating and he rode up to the door of the lean-to and said, "Thank you, Miss Sally, for feeding my horse."

She appeared in the doorway for an instant, very cooly said, "You're welcome, I'm sure," and went back.

He rode off, wondering what had happened in the one day he had been out of circulation. He rode toward the ferry, made out a small dust cloud two or three miles north, and thought it would be Logan. He heard a galloping horse behind him, and turned the sorrel to meet Roy Ernest, long legs akimbo.

"When we goin' to look over Benson's place?" he asked.

"When is the funeral?"

"One o'clock — right after dinner."

Ferguson said, "I want to look over the ferry, and I may have to go across the river. Let's put off going to Mr. Benson's place until after the funeral."

"All right with me. I don't reckon he left much anyway."

"I doubt it — but I thought we might find the address of a relative who ought to be notified."

Another rider came from cross-country, and Black Gallagher pulled alongside. "So far," he said, "we haven't found hide nor hair of Keller. We scoured the river-bottom all day yesterday, and I rode the bank this morning for five miles, lookin' for tracks where he might have gone to water."

"He may of gone acrost," said Ernest.

"It would be the intelligent thing to do — and for that very reason I have no faith in it. I don't think Keller is a man who will do intelligent things."

"You think he's still on this side?" asked Ernest.

"I wouldn't be surprised."

"I don't like the idea of a man like that runnin' loose," said Gallagher, "but I don't know what to do about it until we git our hands on him. *Then* I know."

"I would think," said Ferguson, "that it is best that the women should not be left alone too long, especially at night."

"What about Mrs. Talbot?" asked Gallagher.

Ferguson looked at him. "Has anybody seen her lately?"

"She was in at Turner's about noon yesterday," said Ernest. "Bought a pint of sugar."

"She's probably all right," said Ferguson.

They reached the top of a low hill and on the opposite hill two men worked with pickax and shovel in a hole about knee-deep. Ferguson frowned. "What's that for?" he asked.

"Benson's grave," said Ernest. "He liked the ferry so much, we thought that's where he ought to be planted — and you was not around."

"It's fine with me," said Ferguson.

They rode up to the digging site. Nosey Porter wiped his forehead on his sleeve, and Job Sye sat down for a moment on the edge of the grave.

"Sure is hard ground," said Porter. "When we git through hangin' the feller that did it, I move we throw his body to the coyotes and save all this diggin'."

Ferguson looked at the hole, and a great heaviness came over him. Then Obie Turner came up the slope driving a span of mules. "Mr. Ferguson," he said, "we're movin' sheep. We already got three loads acrost this morning."

Ferguson rode on down the slope. The two Mawson boys were holding some three hundred sheep on the grass flat south of the ferry. Noah, near the ferry, was building up the fire under the coffee. Midway in the river and moving slowly toward the Nebraska side was the ferry, loaded with bleating sheep. Noah walked up to meet him, and asked, "How's the well, Mr. Ferguson?"

"I dug it out on the south side," he said, dismounting, "and it began to run. It might be a pretty good well."

"Fine. Like some coffee?"

"Sure." He took the tin cup and sipped it slowly, thinking it utterly fantastic that nobody had asked him where he had been for almost twenty-four hours. He would not ask what was wrong — not yet.

CHAPTER XIX

THE FERRY CAME in. Noah jumped aboard to get the snubbing-rope, Obie was heard loudly whoaing the mules, and the sheep set up a renewed cacophony of protest.

Obie came down to help, and he and Noah, using the Judas goat, got the sheep off with little delay. Then Noah signaled Teddy Root to take the ferry back. Ferguson watched it go, sensing something strange about it but unable to figure out what it was. He turned to watch Ackerman trot up on his little buckskin.

"Ferguson, glad you're back. Suppose you've heard about Keller."

"Some."

"We sure scoured the country."

"I take it nobody has seen him."

"If they did, they sure kept quiet about it."

"He may have lit out west," said Ferguson.

Ackerman got down. "Sure looks like it to me."

Ferguson looked up toward the men working on the grave. "What do you know about the Otos?"

Ackerman shook his head. "Thirty-five or forty of 'em had a stomp-dance up near the Forks last night. It might mean a war party."

"Was Walking Bird among them?"

"Never heard no mention of him," said Ackerman.

"We'd better keep an eye on those Indians," said Ferguson, "and I have a feeling Keller is still in the country. Let's don't get careless."

"I don't aim to," said Ackerman. "A lot of members of the claim club was real put out because they was cheated out of a hangin', and some of 'em blamed me for not settin' a guard."

"I wonder why you didn't."

Ackerman looked surprised. "I thought you knowed. Sence they wasn't loadin' no sheep on the other side, Bill Benson said he would stand guard until we got ready to hang him."

"You mean try him?"

"All the same," Ackerman said practically.

Ferguson reached down for a blade of rye grass. "That puts a different light on it," he said.

"Not much. We figured he might have surprised somebody releasing Keller."

"Maybe so." Ferguson poked the grass blade between two teeth. "One thing bothers me: it would take a mighty strong man to pull up a dead weight from forty feet down."

"Have you looked at the well?" asked Ackerman.

"Not yet."

"Let's go have a look."

Ferguson caught up the sorrel, and they rode to the well, a hundred feet or so in front of Turner's. They dismounted and went up slowly, examining tracks. "You can't tell much here now," said Ackerman.

"No. Too many men and horses have been over it." Ackerman looked down the well. "No windlass here, but they did build a stone curbing. Mr. Ackerman," he said abruptly, "what kind of rope was Keller let down with?"

"Three-quarter-inch hemp. Why?"

Ferguson pointed. "Hemp threads sticking to the edge of the curbing — and soap smeared along the edge. Did anybody find the rope?"

"Nobody said so. What does it mean?"

"Anybody with a good horse could have tied Keller onto the rope from the saddlehorn, and pulled him up to the edge, then cut his arms free, and the rest was easy."

"But they had to cut Bill Benson's throat first."

Ferguson's jaw was hard. "It looks that way," he said.

Ackerman mounted. "I'll mosey back up to the Forks and keep an eye on the redskins while you rassle sheep."

"See you later," said Ferguson.

He watched Ackerman ride off, and then looked toward Turner's. He saw no one, and mounted the sorrel and rode slowly up the road a way, then looked back. Sally was drawing water, and he was tempted to offer help, but thought better of it, and rode slowly back to the ferry.

Noah was stretched out on the ground near the fire, and Obie was sharpening a jackknife on his cowhide shoe. Across the river the ferry was still tied up, but it was empty, and there was no activity at all on the other side.

"There hasn't been no load sence you was here," said Noah. "We been waitin'."

"I'll go across and have a look," said Ferguson.

He rode the sorrel into the water, and presently reached a point from which he saw a dozen or so men working upriver from the ferry, using shovels at the river bank as if they might be going to cut out a road into the river for a ford. He shook his head over that; it was not feasible to ford the Missouri, even if it were possible — which he doubted.

He reached the sand bars on the far side and rode on them to the scene of activity, where they were indeed making a sloping runway. He rode out onto the bank, identifying three of the men who had been behind Sledge and came face to face with Mawson on a big horse.

"What are you making?" asked Ferguson.

Mawson stared at him with a half-smile on his face. "Just what it looks like," he said.

"You can't ford wagons across this river."

"Who says I can't?"

"You would have to calk the wagons and float them across, but it will still take ropes and men and teams to keep them going west."

Ferguson went down to the dock, and the Reverend Sledge came out to meet him.

"He brought sheep up here." Sledge pointed.

"But he hired away all the emigrants who were helping me — one dollar a day and free passage."

Ferguson said, "Let's recruit more."

"I did, and he hired them. The man is a veritable apostle of evil genius."

Ferguson nodded. "Maybe I could hire them back."

"I doubt it, Mr. Ferguson. On the whole, the people are angry with you for taking the sheep in the first place."

"I had no choice," said Ferguson.

"I know," Sledge said sadly.

Ferguson said, "It will take only one attempted crossing to break Mawson's spell — but that will be too late to help me." He spoke to Teddy Root. "Keep an eye on things, Mr. Root."

There were almost a hundred booted, droopy-hatted men and sunbonneted women gathered for the funeral. Yeakel was there, rather conspicuous in a shiny black suit, and at his side was Wiggins, his arm still slung up; it did not appear, thought Ferguson, that Wiggins was much concerned about the fate of his family.

Reverend Sedge was present, fresh from a big dinner at Ernest's, in overalls and checked shirt and big hat, but with his boots freshly blacked; and Ferguson was glad for those small marks of respect shown by those who had come — even Yeakel.

Sledge preached a long and sonorous sermon at the front door about the forces of evil and damnation, and finally they took the rough board coffin on their shoulders — Ferguson and Yeakel among the six — and marched in slow and mournful procession across the prairie while the women sang "Rock of Ages" and "Jesus, Lover of My Soul." The women had painted the coffin with stove blacking, and it came off when Ferguson's hands got sweaty from the heat and the exertion, but presently they reached the grave where it overlooked the Missouri and the ferry itself. They set down the coffin, and Nosey Porter, who was acting as undertaker, did not open the box at all, but got Ernest to help him pass the reins under it while the Reverend Sledge, bareheaded and Moses-like in the sun, put on some of his best oratory. Then he bent down and got a handful of Nebraska dirt. He arose and began to intone:

Ashes to ashes, and dust to dust — while he let the dust slowly dribble through his fingers.

The six men got hold of the reins, lifted the coffin, poised it over the grave until Porter whispered: "Let 'er go." The women began to cry, and the Reverend Sledge began to pray. Porter and the grave-digger began to shovel in the clods.

Ernest plucked at Ferguson's sleeve, and Ferguson followed him to one side. "What about lookin' over his stuff now?"

"I want to," said Ferguson, "but two Indians have just ridden up to the dock down there, and I think one of them is Walking Bird. Can we put it off for a little while?"

"I'm in no hurry," said Ernest.

"Don't go too far away until I find out what they want."

He went down to the fire, where Noah was making coffee for the Indians. Walking Bird said gravely, "Mr. Ferguson, we have come to help."

"Only two of you?"

"This is Mac Fresh Water. We call him Mac because his father was named Mackenzie."

Ferguson nodded.

"The Otos have split up into two bands," said Walking Bird. "Twenty-four have come with me, to follow the ways of peace, but thirty-four have gone with Rain in July, who is urging them to make war on the whites. He is telling them they can't win, but he has persuaded some of them it is better to die fighting than to live in subjection to Washington."

"Maybe it *is* better — for him."

Walking Bird shook his head. "It may be better for some, but what about the rest of us, who want to live and try to get along with the whites?"

"Of course you will all be Indians when the shooting starts."

"Maybe it won't start," said Walking Bird. "Meantime, I have recruited my men, and we are ready to help you with your sheep."

"I don't see but two of you."

"The others are waiting in the brush along the river until I tell them to come out." Walking Bird grinned sorrowfully. "You know what so many Indians would do to the whites."

Ferguson nodded slowly. "I am going back up to the funeral," he said, "and tell them that you are going to help me, and urge them to preserve order. Then I think you will be safe."

He reached the grave just as the men were tamping the dirt with their shovels, and spoke to the Reverend Sledge, who said: "Brother Ferguson has an important announcement."

The women stopped crying, and Ferguson told them all: "Walking Bird, the Oto, has recruited a band of Indians to help with getting the sheep across the river. These are peaceful Indians, and will do no harm to anybody, but I understand there is a band near the Forks that may give some trouble. Walking Bird's band, however, is peaceful, and I ask your help to preserve the peace. These are good Indians, and they know they are risking their lives to come here in a body, but I have assured them you will respect their offer to help. I would like assurance from you that you will leave them alone as long as they leave you alone."

"I am sure, Brother Ferguson," said Sledge, "that no good Christian man or woman would touch a hair of an honest Indian's head."

"How do the rest of you feel?" asked Ferguson.

Roy Ernest spoke up: "Mr. Ferguson, we know there are some good Indians and some bad Indians, but how are we going to tell them apart?"

"The Indians at the ferry," said Ferguson, "will be Walking Bird's band, and I will be responsible for them. I will personally guarantee that Walking Bird's Indians will do no damage to anybody, and I will warn them to stay close to the ferry."

Gallagher said, "I can get together a bunch of men to act as guard if you want me to."

"Good idea," said Ferguson. "You can keep an eye on both sides — and I don't think there will be any trouble from these Indians."

"Hey," Hudson said, "here comes Logan leading an Indian now."

"No Horse!" said Roy Ernest.

They rode up from the river, horses and clothes dripping, and Logan seemed astonished when he saw the funeral crowd. He started to change his course, but it was too late. Ferguson stepped out to confront him. "Where you going with that Indian?" he asked.

Logan said, "I'm going to hang him for the murder of Bill Benson."

"Without a trial?"

"An Injun don't need a trial."

"How do you know he did it?"

"I found him with a knife."

Ferguson looked at No Horse. The boy's bronze face was impassive, but his eyes showed fright; they changed as he met Ferguson's eyes, and implored him to help. No Horse's hands were tied behind him and a rope around his waist was fastened to the saddlehorn before him. Ferguson asked, "Did you have a knife?"

No Horse nodded yes.

"Did you kill Mr. Benson?"

No Horse looked at the people around him, at Ferguson. "I would not hurt Mr. Benson," he said finally. "He was my friend."

"An Injun doesn't have no friends," said Logan.

Ferguson said, "Since you have brought No Horse for trial, we will take charge of him now, and see that he *gets* a trial — a fair trial."

Logan looked at him quickly. "He's my prisoner," he said.

"The claim club is the only organized law in this region," said Ferguson. "We'll take over the prisoner."

A pistol appeared in Logan's hand. "I brung him here to hang — not to be tried," he said.

"Why? Is it something personal between you and him?"

Ferguson did not want to reveal Logan's true reason until the trial.

"It don't make no difference," said Logan. "If he's guilty, he's goin' to hang."

Gallagher said from behind Logan, "I got a rifle on you, Logan. Put that six-shooter back into your pocket and ride away slow — and leave No Horse behind you."

Logan's eyes shifted for an instant; then he looked at Ferguson and his lips were tight. Slowly he put the pistol into his waist-band.

Ferguson said, "Come around tomorrow night for the trial, if you have any evidence." Ferguson untied the rope from around No Horse's waist and released his hands. "Give me your word you will not try to run away before the trial," he said, "and you can go help Walking Bird."

"I will not run away if you will speak for me," said No Horse.

"Suit you?" Ferguson asked Gallagher.

"Suits me fine."

Ferguson went back to the river with No Horse, while Ackerman got half a dozen men to stand guard along the river bank north of the ferry landing. When Ferguson reached the spot where they kept the fire for the coffee, Walking Bird rose out of the brush. "My men are here," he said.

Ferguson said, "Good. Will you be responsible for No Horse until tomorrow night?"

Walking Bird looked at No Horse. "You stay," he said.

No Horse nodded. "I stay."

Walking Bird said, "You ready to move the sheep?"

Ferguson nodded. He had the ferry pulled back to the Nebraska side, loaded all the Indians on it, along with Noah and Obie, and signaled Teddy Root to pull them across.

Mawson met him on the Iowa side. "What are you up to now?" he demanded.

"I'm going to move your sheep," said Ferguson. "Get them down here."

"You ain't goin' to turn my sheep over to no Indians," said Mawson.

"I made a deal with you to move your sheep," said Ferguson. "Get them down here or I will send men of my own to move them to the river."

He knew the Indians could round them up in better shape, but he was afraid some of Mawson's men would start trouble.

Mawson said grudgingly, "You pay for what you lose."

"That was agreed at the beginning," said Ferguson. "Get them down here."

Mawson glowered, but by mid-afternoon some fifty-five hundred sheep were moving in from the hills. The Otos had stationed themselves to form a fan-shaped chute with a broad apex at the river, and Ferguson soon found that the Indians could handle sheep better than any white man, for in spite of the sheep's being pretty well choused up by Mawson's men, the Indians quieted them and began to form them into a big band, moving slowly toward the river. The Judas goat stepped out ahead, and presently the sheep began to enter the water and spread out far enough to have room to swim. The Indians went into the water with them, and presently, like a miracle, the river was filled with woolly bodies. Ferguson looked at the sheep in the meadow and then at the sun, and said, "We'll have them across by dark, it looks like now."

Sledge, who had been watching, said, "Those Otos sure talk sheep language."

Ferguson watched Walking Bird on the north side and Mac Fresh Water on the south, each with his own crew of Indians, push the sheep into the river, get them across and out on dry land, and headed for the holding-area, where Mawson, obviously against his will, now had his boys and most of his herders to receive the sheep and keep them moving west to make room for others. Ferguson stationed Noah and Obie on the Nebraska side to see that the sheep were moved away from the shore as fast as they reached it, so as not to have a jam in deeper water where the sheep would drown. Mac Fresh Water, on the downstream side, had one Indian watching for strays, and by six o'clock Ferguson could see the end. There were, he estimated, no more than twenty-five hundred sheep left on the Iowa side, and the tables were completely turned on Mawson, who now was fully occupied taking care of the sheep that were delivered to him. Ferguson began to feel exultation as he rode in shallow water alongside Walking Bird. Below him, the river bed was filled with a mass of woolly backs, in a slow moving stream perhaps fifty to a hundred feet wide.

Ferguson looked at Walking Bird, dripping

wet from just having swum across the deep water, and said, "You're doing a fine job. I'll pay all your men a bonus when we get through."

Walking Bird smiled, and at that moment Mac Fresh Water waded through the muddy stream and said to Walking Bird: *"Nih mock-scheh."*

Walking Bird frowned and studied the shoreline. "He says the water is rising," he told Ferguson.

Ferguson felt a sudden emptiness. There were at least two thousand head of sheep in the river, and a fast rise could wipe him out. He looked to the northwest, but saw no clouds.

Mac Fresh Water pointed to the first muddy bubble floating by, *"Han-ua nowai,"* he said.

"It comes from a rain two days ago in the mountains," Walking Bird explained.

Ferguson looked upstream, observed the roily surface, the little rafts of twigs and leaves. He turned away, feeling defeated and suddenly without hope, and rode back to the Iowa shore as fast as he could without creating a disturbance among the sheep.

"Stop them," he told Teddy Root. "The river is coming up. You will have to hold all that are left until the river settles down."

"Do my best," said Root.

Sledge came up. "Couldn't we start moving wagons across on the ferry?"

Ferguson said, "I'm sorry reverend, we've got

255

our hands full. Once we get these sheep across, we'll take wagons — and you will be first. Until then —"

"Mr. Ferguson!"

The hail came from downstream, and Black Gallagher on his horse splashed through the water and up to Ferguson. "Just came from the Forks," he said. "Rain in July's braves are startin' this way."

Ferguson thought about it for a moment. "We'll have to head them off," he said, "and we can't do it with force. When will they get here, do you suppose?"

"Way they was movin', about two or three hours."

"I'd better go meet them."

"I'll get together a dozen men with rifles to go with you."

"No, I want just one man — unarmed. There must be no killing. We must settle these things with talk."

"A man can't talk very good against a tommyhawk," said Gallagher.

"I'm going to try."

"All right," Gallagher said slowly. "I'll go with you."

They rode back across the river and up the slope, into Simon Hudson on a lathered horse. "Feller said to tell you," he said between harsh breaths, "that the Otos under Rain in July went into camp about two mile this side of the Forks, and it looks like they'll be there all night."

Ferguson nodded, then looked at Gallagher. "Maybe we better wait till they start moving again."

"They could change their minds and go back," said Gallagher.

"Can you get somebody to go with you and keep an eye on them?" asked Ferguson.

Hudson nodded affirmatively.

"No shooting, no argument. Stay out of sight, and report to me when they break camp and start moving."

"I'll do 'er," said Hudson.

Ferguson spoke to Gallagher. "We can go back and wait until they move."

"Yeah," said Gallagher. "They *might* move the other way."

Ferguson rode back to the river. Specks of foam and little branches of twigs and leaves were coming down on the brown water, and the level had risen an inch above its previous height. He looked at the twenty-five hundred sheep still on the Iowa side. He hardly dared to use the ferry while the river was up, for a sudden surge would break the guiderope and sweep the raft away from them. He watched Walking Bird's Otos melt into the brush along the river, and Walking Bird stopped for a last word. "We will be back when the river goes down," he said.

"How long will that be?" asked Ferguson.

"Who knows? Maybe a few hours, maybe several days."

CHAPTER XX

FERGUSON SENT ACKERMAN and his guards home for some sleep while he and Gallagher slept on blankets at the dock. In the twilight, the freshly covered grave of Bill Benson made a dark mound against the western sky, and Ferguson was quiet with his own thoughts, but in a moment, tired beyond feeling, he was sound asleep. . . .

He was awakened by the thunder of hooves, and then Simon Hudson was bending over him. "Mr. Ferguson, they're comin' this way!"

Ferguson sat up and began to pull on his boots. "Just started?" he asked.

"Not too long ago. They was camped about six mile northwest. They had a big pow-wow this morning, and they wasn't movin' very fast, but they started towards the ferry."

Ferguson shook Gallagher and got him awake. The river had risen almost two feet, and now was a broad, swirling, turgid mass of brown water. Ferguson reflected that this was the last day he had to get the sheep across, and then threw the saddle on the sorrel and mounted. He rode up the slope past Mr. Benson's grave and paused for a moment, then kicked the sorrel into a trot.

But in the stillness of the early morning he heard more hoofbeats, and saw a rider coming from the direction of Turner's road-ranch, and heard the faint call: "Mr. Ferguson! Mr. Ferguson!"

He did not like the panic in Noah's voice, and he turned the sorrel that way.

Noah was coming at a hard lope. "Mr. Ferguson, Sally's gone!"

"Gone?"

"She got up early," said Noah, "to build a fire. I was roundin' up the mules over the hill when I heard her scream, and then it sounded like a fight. I run back up the hill to help — but she was gone."

"Where was your pa?"

"Him and Obie had went southwest to look for buffalo chips and wood."

"Weren't you on the lookout for Indians?"

"We knew they was camped. Anyways, Mr. Ferguson, it wasn't Injuns. The dirt was all tore up around the well, and there was bootprints."

Ferguson went cold. "What kind of bootprints?"

"Hard to tell. You better come and look." Noah was about to cry. "You will find her, won't you, Mr. Ferguson?"

Ferguson started off toward Turner's, trying to conceal the shock that Noah had given him. Sally gone — kidnaped.

"Mr. Ferguson," said Gallagher, "you're forgettin' the Otos."

Ferguson called back. "Sally's gone! The Otos can wait."

"They won't wait — and they'll kill a lot if they get started. Just let one Injun taste blood —"

Slowly Ferguson turned the sorrel, feeling a great weight in his stomach. He looked at Noah and said, "I will have to go to the Indians first. Get hold of Ernest and Job Sye and organize posses. Tell them not to go around the well, but to wait until I get there. Meantime, tell the posses to scour the country. I should be back within three or four hours, and we will make a careful search. Tell your father not to worry." He put an arm across the boy's shoulders, "And don't you worry. Sally's all right. We'll get her back in good shape. Now go on down to Ernest's and tell him to get organized."

"Yes, sir." Noah turned away. Then he turned back, and his lower jaw was quivering. "You don't think anything happened to Sally, do you, Mr. Ferguson?"

"I don't think so," said Ferguson. "Now run along."

Noah headed south; Ferguson and Gallagher went northwest.

They came in sight of the Otos within an hour. The Indians yelled and galloped toward him, but Ferguson and Gallagher held fast, their right hands upright. The Otos bore down on them, but Ferguson waited until they were close, and then called out: "Rain in July! I want to talk to you!"

The Indians did not slow down, but began to circle, and still Ferguson and Gallagher held fast, and again Ferguson called out to Rain in July, and again there was no answer.

Gallagher, sitting quietly in his saddle with his hands crossed on the saddlehorn, said, "It don't look so good, Mr. Ferguson. They're workin' up their nerve."

"I'm surprised, they have not attacked before now," said Ferguson. He raised his voice. "Rain in July, I want to talk to you."

The circling Indians slowed down, and there was a confab beyond the circle. Then Rain in July rode through his men. "What do you want, Ferguson?" he asked.

"I want to know why you are on the warpath?"

"Because we are hungry."

"Scalps won't get you food. Scalps will get you bullets, and some of your wives will be left without husbands, and some of your children will get more hungry than they are now."

Rain in July showed no emotion. "They are hungry now. What's the difference — hungry or more hungry?"

"If you get killed," said Ferguson, "your wives will have to sell themselves to renegade white men to get food. Do you want that?"

Rain in July said angrily: "We will kill all the goddamn' white men in the world."

"You cannot. There are too many. They will come on and on like the aspen leaves in the fall. There is no end. You kill ten, and a hundred take their places. But there are not many Otos. If ten of you get killed, there will be only twenty-four left."

Obviously Rain in July was not too sure of himself, for he was willing to argue. "We are not many," he said, "but we can die bravely."

"Is it more important to die bravely," asked Ferguson, "or to live for your families? The Indian agent will get your land straightened out some day, and you will be able to live respectably."

"And have a white man come in the way that black-bearded one did, and take us out at the point of a knife?"

Ferguson heard the muttering on all sides. "Do you mean No Horse?" he asked.

"No Horse — he never hurt anybody. Too turkey-hearted to hurt anybody. But the *ma-song-ka* came with a pistol and took him from his lodge."

Ferguson saw his chance. "If I produce No Horse for you, will you drop your scalping knives and go back home?"

"You cannot."

"I can. No Horse is with Walking Bird right now."

"It is a lie!" said Rain in July.

"No. It is true. No Horse helped Walking Bird move the sheep. He is free now."

"I do not believe it."

"Go down along the river and find Walking Bird; there you will find No Horse also. Ask him."

The Otos began to talk among themselves,

and finally drew off, while Ferguson and Gallagher patiently sat their horses, not wanting to move for fear of taking the Otos away from their council.

After a while, Rain in July came up to Ferguson. "We know you are white man who talks straight. If you say No Horse is with Walking Bird, we will believe you."

"He is."

Rain in July searched his face, then nodded slowly, "All right, we go back."

"Let me ask you one question."

Rain in July grunted, and Ferguson knew his life was in the balance; if the answer to the question was yes, they would kill him. But he asked it:

"Did any of your men take a white girl this morning — the girl at Turner's road-ranch?"

Rain in July's eyes opened wide, and Ferguson knew what the answer would be:

"We have not left our camp all night."

"All right. Now go down to the river and join Walking Bird. He is keeping his men hidden until the water goes down. If you join him, and don't cause trouble, I will protect you as much as I can."

"All right," said Rain in July. "But if you fool us, Ferguson, I will cut your heart out with my knife."

"I am not fooling you."

"Go back, then."

Ferguson turned the sorrel and kicked it into

a trot. Gallagher followed him. They rode for a quarter of a mile and went down into a draw, and Gallagher finally took off his droopy hat and slung water from his forehead. "It was close, Sandy John."

" 'Close' doesn't take your scalp," said Ferguson thankfully.

"Do you think they were telling the truth about Sally?"

"I hope so," said Ferguson. "As well as I could, I counted them, and got thirty-four, so they probably were all there."

The horses had slowed down to a walk, and now jogged along, cropping at grass. "As soon as we get over the next hill," said Ferguson, "let's high-tail it for the river."

"Suits me fine. I don't like them Otos behind me so close."

He found Walking Bird near the ferry, and asked: "Who's your best tracker?"

"Mac Fresh Water can follow anything that leaves a track," said Walking Bird. "You want him?"

"Yes."

Walking Bird emitted a call that sounded like a coyote's yapping, and presently Mac Fresh Water appeared.

"I want you to come with me to find a girl who was kidnaped this morning," said Ferguson.

Walking Bird looked at him. "I thought those men were looking for Indians."

"No — the girl, Sally Turner. A man abducted her. They heard her scream."

"I go," said Mac, "if you protect me."

"There won't be any trouble like that." Ferguson asked Walking Bird, "Do you know anything at all about it?"

"Nothing."

"You can ride behind me," said Ferguson to Mac Fresh Water.

When they reached the road-ranch, Turner was making a circuit of the house, looking for tracks and carrying the shotgun, while Obie and Noah, wide-eyed and fearful, watched him from a distance. Turner looked up, distraught. "If I get my hands on him," he said in a tight voice, "I will fill him full of buckshot."

Ferguson motioned to Mac, and led Turner to the door and went inside with him. Mac went to the well and examined the ground; he talked to the two boys; and finally he began to cast wider and wider loops about the cabin.

Turner sat stiff, the shotgun on the table before him, his eyes staring straight ahead.

Presently Mac came to the door. "I know who took her," he said.

A strange and chilling premonition ran over Ferguson. "How do you know?" he asked.

"Tracks. A boot with a spot burned in the sole. I have seen that track before, in Iowa." He motioned with his bare, brown arm.

"A white man, then?"

"Yes. White."

265

Although he did not foresee the exact answer, Ferguson dreaded it, but he finally asked again: "Who?"

"Man name Keller," said Mac.

"Keller!" shouted Turner.

Mac was silent.

"He swore to get revenge," said Ferguson slowly. "Which way did he go?"

"He went into the road. No tracks left."

"Which way?" asked Ferguson.

"Toward ferry."

"Do you think you can find out any more?"

"I can follow road and find out where he left it, maybe."

"By all means, do so. Here's a ten-dollar gold piece for you."

Mac Fresh Water shrugged. "I no track for money. I track because I like you and girl too."

Ferguson put a hand on his shoulder. "Then see if you can find out where the man left the road, so we'll know which way to look. Gallagher, you go with him so nothing will happen to him. I'll be down at the ferry."

He ran into Ackerman with four men behind him. Ackerman said, "We sure looked everywhere."

"Have you seen any sign of Keller?"

"Nope. You think —"

"Mac Fresh Water examined the tracks and said it was Keller — called him by name."

"Holy Jee-rusalem!" said Job Sye. "You know what that means?"

Walking Bird came up. "Water going down now," he said. "Pretty soon we try again, if you say so."

Ferguson nodded. "I say so."

Roy Ernest came down with Nosey Porter, and Ferguson said, "I guess we might as well look in on Mr. Benson's belongings while we're waiting."

Job Sye said, "There's nothin' more we can do. We switch-whipped every barn and out-house in the country. There ain't nothin' we missed. I figure he has gone on west."

"He wasn't that patient," said Ferguson. "He must he hidden out somewhere."

"What we need," said Ackerman, "is a blood-hound."

"We've got one: Mac Fresh Water. He's with Gallagher."

"I know that Injun," said Grimes, "if he can't find her, nobody can."

Ferguson said to Ernest, "Come on, we'll go over Mr. Benson's things."

"Suits me."

"Has anybody checked the Iowa side?" asked Ferguson.

"Ain't had time," said Ackerman.

"Maybe you had better take a look down the shore."

"Do you know any better idea?" asked Ferguson.

Ackerman said, "We'll go have a look."

They rode off into the water, angling up to

allow for the heavier current, while Ferguson and Ernest rode toward Bill Benson's cabin.

When they drew up close, Ferguson said, "There's a horse in the corral."

"A bay," said Ernest, "you reckon Mrs. Talbot come over here to look around?"

"I don't know why she should."

"Been there some time, looks of the droppings."

Ferguson dismounted and rapped on the door. "Anybody in there?" he called.

There was no answer.

Ferguson frowned and rapped again, then pulled the latchstring and pushed the door in.

"Keep your hands up!" said Keller's voice.

Ferguson raised his hands slowly while his eyes adjusted to the inside of the dim cabin. Then he saw Mrs. Talbot, lying half-dressed on a buffalo robe on the floor in the corner. In the other corner was George Keller, no longer handsome in his Eastern clothes, but filthy and repulsive, his hair matted like the hair of an animal, his feral eyes glittering with an evil light as he centered a six-shooter on Ferguson's chest.

"What happened here?" asked Ferguson.

Mrs. Talbot suddenly sobbed. Ferguson looked at Keller and saw the mad light in his eyes as he started to pull the trigger. Ferguson threw himself at the floor, and at the same time was aware that for some reason the door slammed violently behind him.

Keller pulled the trigger, and the room blossomed with white smoke. Ferguson rolled against Keller's legs, and felt the man fall. Then he heard a clank, and looked up to see Sally with both hands on a skillet, raising it to hit Keller again.

But it was not needed. Keller was limp on the floor, and Ferguson's arms were around Sally, and hers were around him. She began to cry then, and Roy Ernest came through the doorway with a rifle.

Ferguson gently disengaged himself from Sally. "Take him away and tie him so he'll never get loose," said Ferguson. "We'll give him a trial in an hour."

Ernest took hold of Keller's shirt in the middle of his back and began to drag him out. "I'll git a wagon-tongue propped up," he said with satisfaction.

Ferguson turned to Mrs. Talbot. "What are you doing in this?"

She straightened up, and he thought she had aged twenty years. "I got him out of the well," she said, "and we hid by the river, but we had to keep moving to keep from being found. We went to your place because he thought you would be gone. He found you in the well, and cut the rope. I wanted to go across the river, but he wouldn't — and then I found out why. He left this morning to get food, he said, but he brought back Sally." She began to sob hysterically.

Ferguson found a small bottle of brandy and gave her a nip. The question was on his tongue: "Why did you leave me in the well and cut the rope so I couldn't get out?" He waited for her to calm down so he could ask, but she continued to sob, and he knew she had been through a terrible experience. He began to understand also why she had cut the rope: because she had offered herself to him, but he had declined and his affection had turned toward Sally. Scorn and jealousy, he decided. Whatever it was, he was glad Sally did not seem harmed.

Finally, Mrs. Talbot began to talk. "He left me in this cabin," she said, "and then he brought her back. He violated me half a dozen times while he forced her to watch, and finally, just a little while ago, he untied her and told her to start fighting him." She began to sob again.

Ferguson looked at Sally. "Did he hurt you?"

She shuddered and clung to him. "You were just in time, Mr. Ferguson."

He looked at Mrs. Talbot. "I'd appreciate it if you would tell the jury what you just told me."

She nodded, crying, and began to put on her dress. Ferguson turned and went out with Sally at his side. He had never been so shaken, and he wanted to get on his horse before he should fall down.

Mrs. Talbot came out, and Ferguson remembered to go back inside and take a quick look.

He found nothing but a small surveyor's note-book with a few addresses and a couple of double eagles in it.

He put Mrs. Talbot on the bay, and had Sally ride double back to the road-ranch, while he went to the ferry to call in Ackerman and all the men he could find.

The Indians were on the far shore, starting the sheep into the water. Ackerman heard Ferguson's call, and presently half a dozen men, headed by Ackerman and Simon Hudson, swam back across the river and started for Turner's road-ranch.

Job Sye presided, and the trial was short. Mrs. Talbot tearfully told her story, and Sally verified it. Mrs. Talbot also testified that she had lured Mr. Benson away from the well to get Keller out in the first place, but that Keller had cut Benson's throat as soon as he got out.

The jury found Keller guilty of murder and also of strange and unnatural practices, and Job Sye sentenced him to be hanged. Roy Ernest had used a doubletree to prop up a wagon-tongue high enough to get Keller's feet off the ground, and a dozen hands pulled down on the rope that went through the eye at the end of the tongue. Keller's neck was not broken, but he strangled fairly fast, and kicked only a few times.

By that time, it was late afternoon, and Gallagher came up to watch the last of the

271

hanging, and then got Ferguson off to one side and said: "Them Injuns just finished gettin' all them sheep into Nebrasky."

Ferguson looked at him and began to smile. "I'm going to collect from Mawson. Anybody want to go along?"

Everybody present shouted, "Me!" and Ferguson mounted the sorrel and set out, followed by the men.

He came upon Mawson and his four sons, herding the new band of sheep, and Ferguson said, "Mawson, I want my money now — nineteen hundred and twenty dollars, according to our bet."

Mawson looked at the men behind Ferguson, and his bravado was no longer present. "Well, I —"

"Gold or silver, according to the agreement."

"I didn't agree to that," said Mawson.

"Your man did — and he's hangin' by his neck back there and can't testify. But I can. Passage is always gold or silver."

"I — I don't think I have that much."

"You're supposed to have," said Ferguson, dismounting, "or didn't you expect to pay?"

"I — are you trying to frighten me, Ferguson?"

"You can pay me in sheep," said Ferguson, "at a dollar and a half a head."

"That's robbery! That's more than I paid for them!"

"They're worth twice that out here. Give me

a bill of sale," said Ferguson, "for twelve hundred and eighty head."

"I can't —"

"Hold your hosses!" said Simon Hudson, climbing down from his horse. He walked up to Mawson and looked into his face. "You consarned tarnation critter! You're the one that sold me the lots in Logan City, and I said I'd strangle you if I ever saw you. You're the president of the Happy Valley Townsite Company. *I'm goin' to strangle you!*"

And he was at the big man's throat before Ferguson could stop him.

Mawson backed away, trying to shake him off, but Hudson hung on. Mawson beat him on both sides of the head with his huge fists, but Hudson's hold did not weaken. Mawson bearhugged him, but it was Mawson's face which began to turn purple, and he finally shook him loose by falling on him. Mawson sprang up first, and took aim with his big foot for Simon Hudson's under jaw.

Ferguson caught him by the arm. Mawson turned in astonishment, and Ferguson uncoiled his long arms and began to hammer him in the face.

The Mawson boys got into it then, but not for long. Ackerman and half a dozen men swarmed over the boys, and in a few minutes they were down.

In the meantime, Ferguson had his hands full with Mawson. The big man was mean and hard, but Ferguson was light on his feet, and his fists landed like chunks of scrap iron. He kept hitting Mawson in the stomach, and Mawson finally bent over, gasping, and Ferguson straightened him with five or six hard blows to the chin. Mawson began to crumple, went down on one knee, and then fell on his face in the dirt.

Ferguson stepped back, and Simon Hudson darted in and got the man by the throat.

Ferguson pulled him off. "Wait till he signs that bill of sale," he said.

Hudson looked up, bright-eyed. "He can sign one for me too, then."

Sally was washing Ferguson's face and cleaning the wounds from Mawson's big fists. Her fingers were soft and gentle as she sponged his face with warm water. She put butter on it and a bandage, and held it in place with court plaster.

"There, Mr. Ferguson." She unexpectedly kissed him on the lips. "I deserve something for a doctor's fee, don't I?" she asked.

His arms went around her hungrily, and he kissed her again and again, but finally he said: "Sally, I want to know one thing: why didn't you and Obie get me out of the well day before yesterday?"

She stared at him for a moment. "Mr. Ferguson, when that Mrs. Talbot come by here and told me *she* had already let you out, you didn't think I was going to go up there, did you? And when you was out of sight for a whole day, what was I to think?"

It dawned on him then. "Sally," he said earnestly, "I was not with Mrs. Talbot — not even for a moment. She didn't help me out of the well at all."

"How'd you git out, then?"

"That's a long story," he said, "but not with her help."

She only half-believed him. "Mr. Ferguson, if I ever find out you been quizzin' me, I'll make all kinds of trouble for you."

"You won't."

"She said — and I thought —" Sally stopped for a moment, then she told him soberly: "Whatever happened, Mr. Ferguson, you got to know one thing: I'm a woman now. I'm not a girl, and I won't stand for my man to look very long at any other woman, and you can't blame me too much fer not gittin' you out of the well, because I thought — well, I'm a woman now, Mr. Ferguson, and —"

He kissed her soundly.

"You sure are," he said.